THE NEW

From the moment pupil-midwife Sally Ashford encounters Matthew Tregonna, senior registrar at the Princess Beatrice Hospital, sparks fly. So how could she possibly fall in love with Matthew when she doesn't even like him?

Books you will enjoy
in our Doctor–Nurse series

HOSPITAL IN THE MOUNTAINS by Jean Evans
UNCERTAIN SUMMER by Betty Neels
NURSE IN NEW MEXICO by Constance Lea
CARIBBEAN NURSE by Lydia Balmain
DOCTORS IN SHADOW by Sonia Deane
BRIGHT CRYSTALS by Lilian Darcy
NIGHT OF THE MOONFLOWER by Anne Vinton
A BRIDE FOR THE SURGEON by Hazel Fisher
THE DOCTOR'S DECISION by Elizabeth Petty
NURSE RHONA'S ROMANCE by Anne Vinton
THE GAME IS PLAYED by Amii Lorin
DOCTOR IN PLASTER by Lisa Cooper
A MATCH FOR SISTER MAGGY by Betty Neels
HIBISCUS HOSPITAL by Judith Worthy
ROGUE REGISTRAR by Lynne Collins
NURSE AT THE TOP by Marion Collin
STAFF NURSE AT ST HELEN'S by Clare Lavenham
APPLE ISLAND by Gladys Fullbrook

THE NEW PUPIL
MIDWIFE

BY

LISA COOPER

MILLS & BOON LIMITED
London · Sydney · Toronto

First published in Great Britain 1982
by Mills & Boon Limited, 15-16 Brook's Mews,
London W1A 1DR

Australian copyright 1982
Philippine copyright 1982

ISBN 0 263 73778 0

03/0282

Set in 11 on 12pt Times Roman

Photoset by Rowland Phototypesetting Ltd.,
Bury St Edmunds, Suffolk.
Made and printed in Great Britain by
Richard Clay (The Chaucer Press) Ltd.,
Bungay, Suffolk

CHAPTER ONE

'I'M sorry, Sister,' said Nurse Ashford for the third time in half an hour. She glanced at the clock in the small side ward reserved for "ladies in waiting", as the midwifery staff at the Princess Beatrice Hospital called the women who were admitted to the midwifery unit for ante-natal care and observation. Mrs Lucy Trevor smiled and looked sympathetic. She had been in the same bed in that same side ward for nearly two months, hoping that this time she would manage to be delivered of a baby, after a history of miscarriages over a number of years. She knew that every fresh batch of pupil midwives had to bear the edge of Sister Beringer's sharp tongue, whether they deserved it or not.

'I want this trolley out of here and then there are the six o'clock blood pressures to take. I suppose you *can* take a blood-pressure reading, Nurse, or didn't they teach you that where you trained?'

'I've taken blood pressures, Sister,' said Sally Ashford, trying to speak calmly, but wishing that she could answer back and tell that awful woman that Beatties, the name that the regular staff gave to the hospital, wasn't the only place on God's earth where nurses were well trained. It was a mistake, she thought. I should have gone to one of the other midwifery schools, even if they lacked the reputation and the wonderful equipment of the Princess Beatrice. I could have stayed near home and at least have been able to go back to my own room at weekends or whenever I had a long off duty.

Sister Beringer closed the door behind her and Nurse Ashford put the foetal stethoscope and examination tray back on the trolley. A soiled rubber glove went into the bin on the bottom shelf and the used towels were put in a bucket. 'Well, everything seems fine, Mrs Trevor,' she said. 'I'll just take your blood pressure and chart it and then you can rest.'

'Rest . . . that's all I do. Don't think I'm grumbling, Nurse, but that's the most boring thing I can think of, when I feel very well and anxious to get on with preparations for the baby.'

'Are you allowed to knit and sew?'

'I've knitted enough matinée coats and boottees to supply the whole ward, and I know that when I go home, I shan't use them all the time. The nice drip-dry, easy care garments are so pretty and good, and I don't want to have to spend my life washing and ironing.'

Sally Ashford asked Mrs Trevor to roll up her sleeve. She applied the soft bandage of the sphygmomanometer to the plump and healthy arm and pumped up the pressure, listening to the sounds of the pulse through the stethoscope that was a part of the equipment kept on the examination trolley. She glanced at the ill-concealed anxiety on the face of the attractive young woman in the bed and smiled. 'That's better . . . much better than last week.' She put the stethoscope on the trolley and made the bed neat again, arranging the pillows so that Lucy Trevor could reach her bed table without personal effort. Then she pushed the trolley into the corridor and briskly took it to the clinical room for cleaning. It was in use so often that Sister Beringer made a strict rule that no part of the equipment should ever be taken away. At all times, fresh hand towels, a fresh draw sheet and plastic sheeting must be on the bottom shelf with the bucket and closed bin, and a tray with rubber gloves and lubricant with a vaginal speculum must be ready in case a consultant or registrar found it necessary to make a thorough examination of a patient. A foetal stethoscope and a doctor's stethoscope completed the list, and woe betide anyone who took any of those things away for any purpose other than bedside examination.

Sally hummed to herself as she cleared the trolley and replaced the soiled articles with fresh ones. In spite of Sister Beringer, this was the work she wanted to do. Ever since she had received her State Registration badge for general nursing, she had been eager to begin training as a midwife. She hesitated, tempted to use the blood-pressure apparatus from the trolley, but went to Sister's office to get the one used for the round of temperature, blood pressure and pulse rate that was the next stage in the evening's work.

The ward was brightly lit and at one end the colour television showed, of all things, another episode in a fictional nursing series. 'That's all I need,' said Sandra White, a girl in the second bed.

'It's bad enough being here, without having to watch that.'

Sally looked at the pretty, discontented face. 'I'll ask Sister if it can be changed,' she said.

'Don't bother. It's even worse without it.' Sandra looked as if nothing could please her. 'We are only allowed TV for an hour now, so we might as well have it, whatever drivel they put on.' Sally noticed that the girl watched the screen intently all the time she had the thermometer in her mouth, and didn't seem to hear Sally say that her temperature and blood pressure were normal.

The patient in the next bed was more forth-coming. 'Hello, Ducks, you're one of the new girls, aren't you?'

'We came on this ward yesterday, when Sister was off duty,' said Sally. 'I've been in the nursery for a week and now I start to nurse the mothers-to-be. This seems a very happy ward.' She smiled, trying to look away from Sandra's petulance.

'All except her,' said Mrs Joiner. She sniffed. 'No ring and was too late to have it taken away. Girls oughtn't to be allowed to do it.' Sally smiled, won-dering what Myra Joiner's solution to teen-ager's might be. 'Now, take me, Nurse, this will be my seventh. Never lost one and they all seem as healthy as you could wish.' She sighed and heaved her bulky figure into a more comfortable position. 'Wish it was all over, Nurse. Tell you the truth, I was upset when I knew about it. Never thought I'd have another. There's a big gap between this one and my Ernie. Ten years, if you want to know. Got me on the change, the doctor said. I told him it was all very well for him to grin when he told me. Had a nice little job I did, and was just getting things straight at home.'

'But now? Are you glad?'

Myra Joiner smiled. 'Of course I am. Love babies . . . always have. It's when the little perishers get about two I could wish them further. Fingers into everything.' She picked up a book as soon as Sally had finished with her. 'I can look at telly at home—it's on all the time—but this is the first time I've had to read a book for ages.' She winked. 'Told them a good story in outpatients. The last one came in a rush and they had me in a few days early as I said I was frightened.' She chuckled and settled down.

'You're a fraud, Mrs Joiner,' said Sally. She finished the round of the ten beds and peeped into the side ward to see if Mrs Trevor was resting, then went back to the office to return the stethoscope, the blood-pressure apparatus and to put a note on the desk to tell the staff nurse who was now in charge during the sister's offduty, that a relative had telephoned to ask if children were allowed to visit. She listened to sounds of activity coming from the labour room along the corridor and knew that this was no time to bother the staff-midwife with details that could wait.

The ward looked neat and peaceful, full of an atmosphere of calm and hopeful anticipation. Even Sandra was smiling, oblivious to anything but the situation comedy now showing on the television screen. It must be a good feeling, thought Sally, to wait in a safe place, clean and comfortable, looking forward to the arrival of a longed-for child. She remembered some of the wards in which she had worked in general training, when the patients were admitted because they were ill, looking unwell and full of apprehension. In spite of Sister Beringer, she knew that life at Beatties could be one of the high-lights of her nursing career. The hospital had tra-dition, and a kind of soft dignity oozed from the very fabric of the place. 'I take back all I said about you,' she said, softly. 'You're a grand old girl.'

As the evening darkened into dusk, Sally eased the tightly-fitting belt on her cotton uniform dress. It seemed very warm and as she made the last round of the evening, before handing over to the night staff, she noticed that the patients were becoming restless and some had tossed aside the bedclothes. 'I don't know how I kept them on when visitors were here, Nurse,' said Myra Joiner. 'It's terrible hot in here.' She looked up at the high windows now fully open. 'My Ernie was born in a heat wave, Nurse. I said I'd never have another baby, but if I did, it would be born in the snow.'

'Well, you misjudged that one,' said Sally. She asked the assistant nurse to bring ice for the water jugs and to make sure that the ice trays in the fridge were full. 'Nothing worse than having lukewarm drinks when you have to stay in bed,' she said. The staff-midwife came back to the ward, briefly, to see that everything was all right. 'I left a note on the desk, Nurse,' said Sally.

'Bless you.' Nurse Cary smiled and brushed a

strand of damp hair from her brow, trying in vain to push it under the inadequate cap that sat on her fair head. 'One advantage of having pupil midwives is knowing that you are trained staff. That's fine. How is Mrs Trevor? Pressure down . . . good. You really have been a tower of strength this evening. We've been up to our eyes in the labour ward. I haven't had a minute.'

'Nice of you to say so,' said Sally. 'I was beginning to feel like a first-day probationer straight from preliminary training school!'

'Oh, you mean Sister? Don't let her get you down. You'll grow to like her in time.' She grinned. 'She loves her work and is scared stiff that some day she will do something daft . . . or that's what I think. She hates change, too. We get this every three months when a new lot of pupil midwives come. The trouble is that she can never give credit for anyone being efficient unless they are midwives. We've even had a theatre sister doing midder, and she still can't see the similarity between a busy theatre and a labour ward.'

'I like the ward and the atmosphere when Sister isn't around . . . I'll take your word that I'll learn to like her,' said Sally. She shifted her feet. 'Do you think we're in for thunder? It's only the end of May, but it's hotter than most Julys.'

'I know. It was very steamy in the labour ward. I thought it was just in there, but when I came to cool off after the baby was delivered, I found it as bad out in the corridor with the late sun streaming in through the windows.'

'Mrs Joiner is very restless. I can't decide if it's the heat or if she's about to go into labour. She's quite a character, isn't she?'

'I'll take a look at her before I go off. Everything tidy? Send the others off if they've finished and just wait around until the night staff come on. The others worked very late last week and I like to let them off early whenever possible. I have to keep one S.R.N. with me until we're relieved, and you're it for tonight.' She smiled and Sally wished that Sister Beringer was more like her senior staff midwife.

The ward was full of tired rustlings as the over-warm patients tried to find a cool spot between the sheets. Sally wondered what it was like in the ward when one or more of the women came into labour. From the baby ward across the way, she had heard sounds of heavy breathing as women were taken to the labour ward for delivery and she knew that for several hours they would have been in the ward, timing contractions and waiting until second-stage labour was imminent. It must be a very different place from the peace of this evening, she thought, but was sorry for anyone confined to bed during what now seemed to be the beginning of a heat wave.

The clinical room was in darkness now that evening treatments were over. Sally tidied the charts in the office, ready for the night staff to examine them before the first ward round of the night, when the house surgeon or the registrar would come to check that all was well and that there was no woman ready for transfer to the labour ward. Suddenly, the light was switched on and Sally could see the figure of a man in a white coat bending over the trolley that she had laid with all the examination equipment on it. Uncertain what to do, as she didn't recognise the man, she went to the doorway in time to see him rummage under the covering towel and take the stethoscope. He was halfway out of the room before she caught up with him. 'Stop!' she called. Her voice sounded over-dramatic, even to her, and she blushed. The man turned, staring incredulously at the girl with deep chestnut hair and apprehensive green eyes who had dared to call to him.

'And who might you be?' the voice was cold and the blue eyes disdainful.

'That stethoscope never leaves the trolley,' Sally said, with more firmness that she felt. 'Sister is very strict about it. Please give it to me.' He's just a house surgeon, trying it on, she told herself, but inwardly knew that this wasn't just another young embryo doctor on his first house job. This man was older, with the air of authority that experience brings. He gave a short laugh and turned away, striding along the corridor to the labour ward. Sally looked back, but Nurse Cary was nowhere to be seen. She walked quickly after the man who was already placing the ear pieces in his ears. He flung open the door to the labour ward and it swung closed after him, leaving Sally standing helplessly on the other side. What should she do? Every department had its own equipment. The labour ward must have its own supply of stethoscopes, the doctors carried their own with them in the dragged down, capacious pockets of the white coats they wore, so why should he take one from another department?

She went back to the pre-natal ward and hovered in the doorway until Nurse Cary came out of the side ward. 'A man, I suppose he was a doctor, came and took the stethoscope from the examination trolley, Nurse Cary.'

'He *what*? Sister will scream blue murder. I'm not too happy about Mrs Joiner. She's had a couple of twinges. You'd better get that thing back, or Sister will flay you alive in the morning, not to mention Mr Dillinger if he does a round. He never re-members to bring his own things,' she added, cheerfully. 'Ah, here come the night staff. Would you put them in the picture while I have another look at Mrs Joiner, and then you get that steth. back.'

'But I don't know who he is, Nurse. How can I go along and ask the staff if I don't know his name?'

'Medium height, sandy hair?' Sally shook her head. 'Oh, it isn't Mr Dillinger, then. He's our obstetrics consultant. Must have been our Matthew . . . tall, fair and handsome?'

'And supercilious,' said Sally, with feeling. 'Made me feel as if I was something the cat brought in and dropped on the mat.'

'He can be a bit naughty, but nice, don't you think?' She turned to the ward door. 'Give report and go hunting . . . and good luck.'

Sally looked at the retreating back of her senior.

'Have fun!' she said. Remembering the cool indifference of the man with fair hair made her wish she could change places with Nurse Cary. Surely, it would be easier to cope with a woman in labour than to confront that man again. I shall feel such a fool, she thought.

The corridor was empty. Sally tapped on the door leading to the corridor from which the various rooms of the labour ward radiated. She had never been inside the department and wasn't aware that she was tapping on a door that had no entry to a room or office. She waited and tapped again, listening for footsteps. Nothing happened and she slowly opened the door a fraction and peeped inside. Realising her mistake, she went into the short corridor and saw that the doors were labelled. The labour room was at the far end, a recovery room was to one side and an office near the entrance by a room used for patients well on into labour but not ready for the main theatre. The door to the recovery room was partly open and through the gap she could see a gowned and masked midwife, a young medical student and a pupil midwife, similarly clothed, and a tall man with his gown tied badly so that, at the back, it trailed to one side ready to trip him up at any minute.

Sally hung back, knowing that no member of staff must go near a new delivery without being gowned and masked, to prevent the spread of infection from outside the ward. There seemed to be a lot of activity and an air of tension. The tall man straightened and took the stethoscope from his neck, thrusting it into the pocket of the coat he wore under his gown. 'Fine,' she heard him say. 'I don't think we need worry about you . . . but you did give us a moment of panic, Mrs Eaves.' Sally caught a glimpse of a pale face on the pillow and the hand that reached up to clasp the strong fingers that touched her arm with reassurance.

'You've a fine son and you've stopped bleeding. By tomorrow, you'll wonder what all the fuss was about,' said the midwife, and smiled up at the blue eyes that gazed with humour and care at the woman on the bed.

The man left the bedside, tugging at the tapes on the gown. He threw the white cap on to the floor and swore, gently. 'Let me help,' said the midwife. He turned to face Sally Ashford while the girl struggled to untie the knots that he had dragged tight. He stared and lifted one sardonic eyebrow.

'And what do you want now?'

'I came to fetch the stethoscope that you . . . borrowed,' said Sally.

He shrugged out of the gown, leaving it in the grasp of the midwife as if he was used to being waited on. 'And you came here to demand it back —when we were having a slight crisis? Do you always butt in when you're not invited, without having the courtesy to address a member of staff by name?'

She wished that her heart would settle to a beat that didn't sound to her like the tympani of a vast orchestra. How could a man who looked as he did, speak to a girl in that sarcastic tone? The wide and humorous mouth gave the lie to the steely dis-approval in his eyes, but all she could think was that he disliked her and that she couldn't call him by name. Nurse Cary had referred to him as "our Matthew". That was it! Surnames were used ex-tensively in a hospital situation.

'I'm sorry, Dr Matthew,' she said. 'But that stethoscope belongs to Pre-natal. Sister has very rigid rules about it being on the trolley at all times.' She sensed the ripple of amusement from the two nurses who listened, fascinated. The blue eyes darkened and he flung the stethoscope at her, violently, so that it nearly fell to the floor. 'Well!' she said, her anger overcoming her diffidence.

'Don't say another word, Nurse. I see by your uniform that you have honoured Beatties with your presence for three months as a pupil midwife, but let me just say this. At no time do you call a registrar by his first name in an attempt—a feeble attempt—at levity. If I have the misfortune to see you again, which heaven forbid, you will call me Mr Tregonna.'

Sally clutched the stethoscope and almost ran from the department, aware of hostile eyes watch-ing her retreat and the giggles of the nurses.

'I hate it here . . . I was mad to come. I'll chuck it in . . . I'll go home.'

'Well, what brought that on,' said Nurse Cary as she watched Sally put the stethoscope back in its right place. 'Irritable was he?' She grinned. 'Our Matthew can be very naughty, as I said.'

'Our Matthew can go to hell!' said Sally.

CHAPTER TWO

'HERE you are . . . made with real lemons and lots of ice.'

'You just saved my life,' said Sally Ashford. 'Thanks, Charlie.'

Charlotte Davenport regarded her fellow student with amusement. 'I thought I was the one who got in a tizz over people. Who got under your skin today that you come in here spitting blood?' She sat on the arm of the chair and rocked slightly, making the chair squeak and exude tiny puffs of dust.

'It's so hot,' said Sally, putting the empty glass back on the tray and eyeing the equally empty jug with longing.

'Just the heat? Surely you haven't gone through a complete S.R.N. training without having one hot day?'

Sally brushed her deep chestnut hair back from her face and threw the tiny nurse's cap on to the table. 'It wasn't just the heat, although I suppose it made me edgy. I met the most awful man today on Pre-natal. He came in without so much as a polite "may I?" and pinched the stethoscope from the examination trolley. I went after him and he was as unpleasant as any man could be.' The memory of her encounter still caused her to breathe hard, as if she found it difficult to control her temper, but

18

somehow, it wasn't anger that made her heart beat fast and her throat try to close over the words.

'Well, it couldn't be Mr Dillinger,' said Charlotte. 'He's a poppet. He's half American and half English and Sister Beringer even smiles at him, which must be a record, as everyone says that she hates all men.'

'I can't think why she works in midwifery if she feels like that. She has to meet pregnant fathers all the time and having babies is so much to do with love that she must know that she is out of sympathy with such situations. I always thought midwives were plump, motherly bodies with vast bosoms and broad shoulders for crying on.'

Charlotte laughed. 'The complete opposite to our revered Sister Beringer, but I'm beginning to admit that she not only knows her job inside out, but all the patients have great faith in her. In a way, it's better to be detached rather than too sentimental over birth and death.' She took the glasses to the sink in the kitchen of the nurses' home and rinsed them under the tap. She filled an ice tray with fresh water and put it in the freezer compartment of the fridge freezer. 'Everyone will be screaming for ice this evening. It's much too hot to think of going to bed yet, tired though my poor old feet are.'

'I think I'll have a cool shower and come down to make coffee,' said Sally.

'You'll be just as hot again before you go to bed. Keep in uniform and come round the garden with me, then we can cool off before bed.'

They went out into the warm dusk and strolled

beneath the sighing poplars that lined the driveway between the main gate and the exit to the park next door to the hospital. 'We should have changed, then we could go into the park,' said Sally.

'Not worth it tonight, but I shall go and sit by the fountain tomorrow when I'm off. It's very good in the day time and there are masses of shady trees, but it's more than our job's worth to go out there in uniform. That's one of the rules that have to be kept here at Beatties.'

'You're lucky. You know the place, having trained here. I feel as if I was just beginning my training all over again.'

'You're not the only one. Midder is a new training. I'd heard that we became the lowest of the low once more when we started the course, but I didn't realise just how low we rate with people like Sister Beringer. Where did you train?'

Sally told her about Bristol and the hospital in the city where she had taken her S.R.N. because it was close to her home, and although she couldn't live out all the time, she could get away from hospital frequently for off duty and some weekends. Charlotte listened, asking the occasional question, and Sally found that she was making excuses for training so close to home. 'I went away of course, visiting, and I had lots to do in the town. Bristol's a very good centre for entertainment, being a University city. I enjoyed it,' she said, defensively.

'And why not? I'm curious only because I couldn't get far enough away from home to do my training. I was swamped by family and the people in the village and the neighbouring houses. It's true we had riding and lots of parties, but always with the same set, the same dreary men who thought of nothing but horses and money and the women who had nothing better to do than gossip and bitch at every party if one as much as *looked* at a man. Most of them were jealous of anyone who had the chance to escape an early, arranged marriage with a suitable man.' She laughed, but there was bitterness in her laughter. 'Suitable . . . that's really funny. My cousin was pushed into marrying a man with a drink problem who gives her a hell of a life. He was rich and had a title.' She shrugged.

'But surely . . . not now? That went out in the last century. Girls can look after themselves now and support themselves. No one from your sort of background lacks education and opportunity, surely?'

'Surely!' mimicked Charlotte. 'It happens. A girl like me, you say, well, perhaps I had more determination than my cousin. I was a rebel as a child and thank goodness it was never driven out of me. I said I wanted to be a nurse and they all laughed. Then my mother, who has some sense, said it was only fair to let me try, if only to convince myself that nursing was tiring, dirty, unpleasant and lacking in any social contacts with "the right people".'

'And here you are with one certificate behind you and on your way to another. Good for you.' Sally frowned. 'When I first saw you, I envied your clothes and your self-confidence. I had no idea that your family could be so archaic in their outlook. I would have thought there were hundreds of men with looks and charisma as well as money. Going to hunt balls and parties must give you a certain advantage.'

'Yes, but it's double edged. I met men who were everything you mentioned, one or two were mind-bending, but they wanted more than a pretty face and an ability to hand round snacks at parties. Horses were a link, but you can't talk horses for ever. The men I fell for were intelligent and worked hard even if they were rich enough to do nothing but follow hounds.'

'So you decided to train?' Sally looked up through the soft cloud of leaf above them, letting the slight movement of air cool her face. 'I came here to escape, too,' she said, as if admitting it for the first time. 'I love it at home, and I was happy during my training, but I did sometimes wish that I could go out for a day on my own without having to tell my family where I was going. If I didn't go home for days off, they rang to see if I was ill. I once had four days in the Lake District, walking with two other nurses, and you would have thought that we were going to fall down a mountain or be raped!' She smiled in the darkness. 'They really care, but it gets a bit claustrophic. That four days was bliss. We met some students from Lancaster who were hill-walking and they stayed at the same hostel.'

'Aha! Do I scent romance?'

'No. Half the time we were dripping with rain and when we were in the hostel we exchanged aspirin and Vitamin C, not burning glances. But it was fun.'

'Come off it, Sal, you must have boy friends. That hair must be worth its weight in gold. I've never seen such a rich colour, and with green eyes, too. You'd be a riot in the right clothes at one of our shindigs.'

'I go around with a boy from home who is back in Bristol teaching biology. He's useful to have around, but I'm not in love with him.'

'Are you sure?'

'I think so. I've known Brian since I was eleven. I went to a Convent school for girls and he was at the local Grammar School. I suppose I've never quite forgotten that we used to travel on the same bus and hurl insults at each other. In many ways he's like a brother, but my family seem to think we are made for each other.'

'Not much difference between your lot and mine, after all,' said Charlotte. 'Let's form a society of two members to fight families forcing men on us.' They giggled and the next half hour passed quickly as the darkness deepened, bringing a slight respite from the heat. A low rumble of thunder came from the other side of the city and a flash of white light cut through the steady glow that came from the busy West End of London in the distance.

'Poor Mrs Joiner,' said Sally. 'Can you imagine what it is like to be in labour in a thunder storm? She hates the heat and Nurse Cary thought she might be starting tonight. She already has four boys and two girls.'

'Lucky woman,' said Charlotte, seriously. 'I'd like a large family, wouldn't you?'

'I don't know,' said Sally. 'To be honest, I've never considered it. I've been too busy getting trained and coming here. I love babies, but I just can't think of having my own.' She tried to picture herself holding her own child, as if looking at a picture. In the picture there would be the baby's father . . . but Brian wouldn't come into mental focus and the figure was shadowy and the face blank. 'I'm not ready for that. There is so much I want to do . . . so much to see, so many people to meet.' She moved restlessly. 'I thought that I would find all the fulfilment I needed in nursing, and I have, but now, coming away from home is like a new beginning, a fresh start in life, and somehow there is a sense of adventure, of a pre-cognition of excitement that may just mean a different kind of nursing, a different life style . . .' Her voice tailed away.

'We've a lot in common,' said Charlotte. 'We've both escaped from our respective comfortable prisons and we don't even know what we're seeking.'

'I'm not seeking anything,' said Sally, quickly. 'I think I'm excited about the work and delivering my first baby.' But through the leaves above the wooden seat on which they sat, the warm, heavy air sighed of love and an emptiness of heart such as she had never known before. The moon rose, softened by cloud, sending bright shafts of silver through the poplars, and the distant sound of traffic murmured that out there, in the city, was excitement, adventure and romance.

'The moon's come in fine . . . I think we're set for hot weather for a while, whatever the weather pundits tell us. You see, this cloud will go by morning and we'll be baked alive.'

'How can you tell?' said Sally.

'I'm just a country girl at heart,' said Charlotte, stretching legs that even duty shoes and grubby stockings couldn't rob of their elegance. 'I shall have a shower, get ready for the morrow and look out my very best bikini.'

'Bikini? Here?'

Charlotte laughed. 'Not on duty, Sally. I can almost hear Sister Beringer telling me that bikinis are *not* quite what the well-uniformed Beattie's nurse should be wearing, but she would put it more forcefully. No, I've been here long enough to know all the bits in this building that you might never find. I went on a tour when I came here. I know of two windows that are easy to open in the nurses' home, not that it matters now. Since the other hostel was burned down, we have medical staff sleeping in the nurses' home and everyone has to be allowed free access. It's like admitting wolves to a nunnery,' she said, cheerfully, 'but there is very little scandal. I think they work us all so hard that we haven't the energy for anything after ten p.m.'

'A back way in isn't an excuse for a bikini.'

'No . . . I was forgetting. At the back, overlooking the park, is a piece of flat roof with a fairly high surround of low wall. I sunbathed there all through the hot spell last year while I sat for finals. Didn't do much studying, but I got a real South of France sun tan.'

'Are we allowed there?'

'Oh, well, the medics use it so why not us? With all the perks, it's best not to ask, but to take it for granted that it's permitted until you get caught.' She glanced at Sally as they went into the nurses' home. 'Don't look so worried. I think that trained staff are allowed there, and in spite of the dirty looks we get from Sister, remember that we are trained staff, even if we can't yet deliver a baby with one arm tied behind our backs.'

'Who does that? Only Sister Beringer would have that much skill,' said a voice that was deep and amused. The girls swung round to face the man who had followed them through the wide-open doorway. Charlotte treated him to a dazzling smile. 'Are you both as new as I am?' he said. 'I seem to spend my time telling nurses what to do, only to find that they have been here for years and know more about the patients and treatments than I'll know even after my stint here.'

'We're in the new batch of pupil midwives,' said Charlotte. Sally said nothing, but lowered her eyes, hiding them under thick dark eyelashes. He spoke to Charlotte, but his gaze was on Sally, bold and challenging and vaguely disconcerting.

'Well, well,' he said, quietly. 'The Princess Beatrice Hospital is looking up. I'm Dorian Warner, doing six months on a research project— Kernicterus and the prevention of brain damage.'

'So you'll be working in midwifery,' said Charlotte.

'Mostly post-natal, and suspected cases in antenatal where the mother has had one Rhesus-positive baby without being anti-bodied by her own Rhesus-negative blood. We want to monitor these, particularly as they are at greater risk.' He frowned. 'I've been here three weeks and I missed one. She didn't come in until she was well in labour and I had gone away for a day, thinking all was quiet.'

'Was she all right?' said Sally.

'Oh, yes,' he said, as if that was the least of his worries. 'Both did well, and they didn't have to change the infant's blood, but it does mean that I can't claim that case on my records.'

'Does it matter?' Sally was becoming embarrassed by his cool appraisal of her face and figure. 'The important thing was that they were both safe.'

'You wait until you have to stay with a woman in labour, only to have her delivered by another midwife or medical student when you fly off to eat for half an hour. You'll be put out when you find you're short of one official delivery to make up your quota.'

'I'd rather know the baby came safely.' She could feel the blood tinging her cheeks and hated herself for reacting to his masculinity.

He smiled. 'If I had my way, they'd all come in when we sent for them, to be induced when it was convenient for the staff. It could cut down hours of duty and we'd be on hand when needed . . . and I'd get my notes straight.'

'You didn't train here, Dr Warner,' said Charlotte.

'No, I didn't. I've lived abroad for several years and learned a lot in a very progressive hospital, south of the equator, where I received a good training and some very sound ideas.'

'And now you have to take courses to catch up with the men here!' said Charlotte, coldly. 'I've heard of that conveyer-belt kind of delivery and if you value the good opinion of Mr Dillinger, you'll keep those ideas to yourself. He likes to know that his patients come in and have their babies as naturally as possible.'

'You could do away with half the beds in prenatal if you booked them in.'

'What about people like Mrs Trevor? She needs to be at complete rest until her baby is due, to prevent losing it,' said Sally. 'It would upset her very much to see other women coming in and having drips put up to start them in labour before the natural time, when she has to wait and wait, hoping that hers *won't* come too soon.'

'A couple of side wards and isolate the patient,' said Dr Warner, airily, but Sally saw the amused glint in his eyes and wondered how much was cool calculation and how much was teasing, trying to goad them into affronted horror.

Charlotte fanned her face with a copy of the *Lancet* which she took from an untidy pile on the table of the sitting-room. 'Do you think coffee would make me hotter or do you want a cold drink?' she asked Sally.

'You mix a fruit drink and I'll bring something to put in it. A little alcohol will calm those pupil midwife nerves. I think I've some oranges to add to the mixture,' Dorian said.

Charlotte went to her room to fetch the rest of her lemons and Sally remembered a huge orange given to her by a new patient. She fetched it and went to the fridge to get ice, hoping that there was some left. She felt elated, attracted to the good-looking man with the dark brown eyes, in spite of the fact that she didn't like some of the ideas he put forward. At least he's pleasant, she thought. The ice cubes fell into the bowl, with a cool sound. She smiled ruefully. Ice, as if she hadn't had enough ice for one day, from the contemptuous eyes of the man with fair hair and a gown tied as badly as a coat buttoned by a five year old. Her pulse quickened. I shall have to see him again in the wards or in the labour room. What if he recalled the incident when she thought she was calling him by his surname. The memory was still sharp and painful. He must have thought she was trying to make up to him, perhaps even to flirt with him.

'That looks good.' Dorian Warner waved a bottle of dry Vermouth and watched Charlotte squeeze the juice from the oranges and lemons. Sally found a huge pottery jug in a cupboard in the kitchen and filled it with ice and juice and water. Dorian Warner opened the windows of the sitting-room as wide as they would go and put the jug and Vermouth on a table. 'Drag a chair up, I really believe there's a little air here.' Sally pulled at a chair which caught its casters on a rug. Strong hands helped her, and as she straightened from the near crouching position, her face was inches away from the smiling dark eyes of the doctor. 'Even better, close up,' he whispered, and as she tried to stand, endeavouring to move away from him, he swiftly kissed her cheek.

'Dr Warner!'

'Come on, have some liquid,' he said, with a grin. 'Couldn't resist it. Don't be mad at me, you're the prettiest girl I've met since I came here.'

Sally shook her head in mock despair. 'Charlotte warned me about wolves in the nurses' home, but I didn't believe her.' She moved away to pour out the inviting cool drinks, making sure that Dorian Warner didn't have a chance to put too much Vermouth into the glasses. He grumbled that he was in the mood for a party and called her a spoilsport, but his eyes seemed to caress her as she moved about the room.

'A party? Can anyone join in?' A pretty West Indian girl stood in the doorway with a bottle of lime juice in her hand. 'I was coming to see if there was any ice left,' she said.

'Come in, Vi. We haven't used it all.' Charlotte scooped ice and fruit from the jug and insisted that Violet Bastable had as much as the others. She sipped it slowly, her eyes sparkling with pleasure. 'I've been promising myself something like this all evening. It's great, Charlie.'

Dorian Warner looked from one to the other and then at Sally. 'I thought you were all strangers. Aren't you from different training schools?'

'Adversity, that's the common denominator, isn't that so, girls?' Violet's plump shoulders shook with laughter. 'We're so full of sorrow that we cling together for comfort. All friends within five minutes of seeing Sister Beringer.'

'Then you must let me join you.' Dorian advanced towards Violet, took both her hands and said solemnly, 'Dorian Warner, Dorian to my friends, Violet.' He bent forward and kissed her lightly on both cheeks. He repeated the salute with Charlotte who giggled, and turned to Sally, who had the suspicion that he was going through the ritual to come to her. She smiled slightly as he took her hands and she knew that he was slightly drunk. His grip was tight as he drew her towards him, the look in his eyes lacked the humour they held when he kissed the others. He seized her firmly, crushing her lips beneath a kiss that had no tenderness, no friendship, nothing but naked desire. She struggled and pushed him away and fell back against the arm of a chair, losing her balance and toppling into the deep seat, her legs waving wildly as she tried to regain her balance and composure.

'You . . . you beast,' she gasped. To her relief, he didn't follow up his advantage, and the room was suddenly quiet. She looked up after pulling her uniform skirt down from its revealing position round her waist and saw that Dorian was being held in a vice-like grip by a man with angry blue eyes and an impassive face.

'I think the party is over,' said Matthew
Tregonna. 'Don't you think that the night is hot
enough without this kind of exhibition?' He
glanced at the bottle on the table. 'Alcohol isn't
very good for people expected to do a responsible
job the next morning.'

'We weren't drinking,' said Charlotte. 'It's
mostly orange squash. Have some,' she added, im-
pulsively, with an attempt at making him relax and
smile.

'As you were making such a row, I assume that
nobody heard the telephone? Is there a Nurse Ashford here?' Sally nodded and walked slowly
towards him and the door. 'What a busy girl it is,' he
said, sarcastically. 'Men telephoning, and a little on
the side in the sitting-room.'

Sally clenched her hands as she passed him. She
was acutely aware of the man, his strength and
machismo, his dislike; and she knew that she was
fated to see him during her work in midwifery, see
him in the home where he must have a room; and as
she brushed past him, she knew that she must never
come into physical contact with him again. The
touch of his hand, accidentally on her arm, was like
a spark . . .

'Hello,' said Brian. 'You took your time.'

'I was . . . delayed,' said Sally. 'I was called to the
phone while one of the doctors held me up.' She
had an absurd desire to giggle . . . if Brian could
have seen her in the sitting-room chair, would he
sound so quiet, so settled, so uninteresting?

'I miss you,' he said. 'When are you coming home, Sal?'

'I don't know,' she said. 'I have lots of studying to do and we are run off our feet.'

'You've been busy before. What's different?' He went on to tell her news that no longer seemed necessary for her to hear. He told her his golf score and the fact that his father and her father had joined the same snooker club. She let the sounds flow over her and when he said goodnight, she realised that she had said hardly anything.

'I'll let you know,' she said. She walked along the deserted corridor and up the stairs to her room. She flung the window wide and leaned on her elbows over the window sill, putting her face to the cool glass and listening to the sound of an ambulance bell. I'll have to go home soon, she thought. I have to strengthen the ties, not break them. This was a new life, a new beginning, with strange undertones that excited her and filled her with an exquisite dread. The night was dark and timeless, giving nothing back as she silently asked for wisdom. And in her heart, she knew that the stars, the moon and whatever gods there might be would not be able to tell her how to avoid her destiny. She touched her bare arm lightly, not where the passionate grip of Dorian had bruised her flesh, but where the lightest touch of an angry man had made accidental contact.

CHAPTER THREE

'WHERE did you get to? You weren't at breakfast,' said Sally Ashford.

'I went for an early swim. I couldn't sleep as it was so hot, and I have a horror of flying insects in my room at night, so had to keep the curtains drawn.' Charlotte Davenport tossed back her still damp hair and tried to pin her cap more securely. 'You should have come . . . quite a lot of Beatties were there.'

'Nobody asked me,' said Sally. 'You forget that I don't know my way around yet. I didn't even know there was a good swimming pool near the hospital. Let me know when you go again. I'd love to come.' She glanced enviously at Charlotte's cool face. 'It's a scorcher today. The porter said that the woman who sells flowers outside the gates will be spraying yesterday's faded blooms, hoping to convince customers that they are dewy fresh.'

'Oh, take no notice of Claud. He's a conniving old devil. He's useful if you want stamps or something posted in a hurry, but never tell him anything about yourself that you don't want to go round the hospital in the next five minutes.'

'I thought he seemed very interested when I walked down to the gate this morning to try and get a breath of fresh air. He asked me where I lived and said that one or two of the doctors came from

Bristol or from Somerset.'

'Did he say who they were? In my part of the world, men from here are thin on the ground. I'd hoped to get a lift home sometimes, but I haven't had much luck lately since my crowd left.'

'That's a good idea. I know that nurses shared the cost of petrol when they went home from Bristol if they could find someone going in the same direction. Fares are horrendous. Is it allowed to put a chit on the notice board to team up for lifts?'

'Yes, there's a board in the nurses' home. Just put times and dates and anyone interested will add his or her own note to yours.' Charlotte paused at the door to her part of the midwifery complex. 'Don't put a name or you'll get wolves like Dorian literally taking you for a ride!' She went into the nursery, leaving Sally to brace herself for the first meeting with Sister Beringer.

The ward was fairly chaotic, with two patients panting gently as they began the first stage of labour. The windows were wide open, but the air was so still that the curtains hung down as if tethered to the walls. Myra Joiner's bed was empty and made up with fresh linen. 'Has she had her baby?' said Sally to Staff Midwife Cary.

'Mrs Joiner? Oh, yes, she went into labour very quickly and had her babe at midnight. We had quite an argument with her about the time.' Cary laughed. 'She wanted to be able to say it was born yesterday as she already has one son born on this date, but she's unlucky, I'm afraid, five minutes after midnight makes his birthday today. She'll have double birthdays for ever more.'

'That'll be Ernie,' said Sally. 'Where is she?'

'You'll see her soon. I want you to relieve on post-natal until lunchtime. Sister is off this morning and lecturing nearly all the afternoon, so you'll have to put up with me and Nurse Smythe. 'Sally smiled. 'We might be busy, so don't look *too* pleased. Do you have a lecture today?'

'One at three-thirty with Sister Beringer, an hour for notes and off this evening. Sister said she likes to give a couple of lectures before we get anywhere near the labour ward.'

'You realise that she is probably the best tutor in her branch of nursing? You're lucky to have her. When you go down to Surrey for your second three months you will realise just how much she has taught you. Lots of girls come back ready to admit that they misjudged the lady very badly.'

'I'll take your word for it, Nurse Cary. What do you want me to do?'

'Go to post-natal and lay up the trolley for swabbing down for the three deliveries that came yesterday. See to them first and let the juniors clear the lockers and bed tables, check that they have charted any intake on fluid charts, and any urine measurements. Pads go on a tray in the sluice room in case they have to be inspected, babies are given out for ten o'clock feeds unless they are on three hourly or two hourly, when the nurse from the baby room will bring them and take them back.'

Already the list of duties was so long that Sally wondered if she would surface before lunch time, but the atmosphere of the happy ward was infectious and as she brought the newest addition to the Joiner household to her mother, Sally shared in the delight so obvious among the mothers.

'She's lovely, isn't she, Nurse? Do you think she's going to be pretty?' Myra Joiner hitched the baby up into the crook of her arm and wriggled herself comfortably against the pillows.

'She's beautiful,' said Sally, laughing at the crimson, puckered face that looked more like Winston Churchill than a beautiful maiden. 'I'm sure the others will love her. If she's so much younger, and a girl this time, she'll be spoiled by all her brothers and sisters.'

'Well, here goes,' said Mrs Joiner. 'Now my troubles really begin. I asked if I could put her on the bottle, but Sister wouldn't let me.'

'But you look as if you will have plenty of milk.'

'I know. That's never been the trouble, but now, when she starts to suck, I shall go through agonies, Nurse.' Her wide smile lessened the impact of her words. 'Sister said that the baby sucking is the only way to get my womb back to the right size. It's like being in labour all over again, but I suppose I'll have to grin and bear it. Come on, my love . . .' She put the baby to the breast and it was plain that she had done this so many times with her other children that she needed no help or instruction, unlike the young mother in the next bed who sat the baby precariously on her lap and looked at it as if it was something rare and strange.

'Come on, Mrs Chambers, you must try or the

baby will have nothing.' Charlotte, on duty in the baby room, took the baby and held its mouth gently to the young mother, putting a finger under the chin to make the baby suck. 'Now, hold her, like that. I'll put the pillow to support your arm. Relax and enjoy your baby.'

'Rapid promotion,' said Sally as she passed by the bed.

'Yes, the next one up had to replace a nurse in the labour ward who is off sick. I love the babies. I like them as they are here, and not when they are inside, making life miserable for their poor mothers!' She glanced round the ward. 'No doctors yet. I thought they'd finished in the labour ward.' She nodded towards the two empty beds. 'They're in recovery—one breech and one R.O.A. with an episiotomy.'

'Who was on last night?'

'I think there was a bit of a row. Dorian Warner was on duty—he has to do some deliveries as well as getting data for his thesis—but Mr Tregonna said he'd stand in as he thought that Dr Warner was in no fit state to attend the women.'

'Phew . . . that was a bit high handed, wasn't it? Has he the authority?'

'Authority or not, he sent Dorian off to bed and sat up until four until the breech was safely delivered.' Charlotte collected a baby to be weighed to find out if she was having enough from her mother. The baby wailed plaintively as she was put on the scale and Charlotte made a face. 'Another supplementary feed. I'll take her back to the nursery and tell them and come back for the other one.'

Nurse Cary came into the ward and glanced round with practised perception. 'All right, Mrs Joiner?' She swished the curtains round the bed and called to Sally Ashford to take the baby. 'Get her wind up while I examine Mrs Joiner.' Sally put the baby to her own shoulder and walked away from the bed, gently patting the blanket that shrouded the tiny back. The small face had a windy ring round the mouth until a satisfying burp and a return to normal colouring showed that all was well. Hungrily, the baby tried to mouth at Sally's cheek.

'You won't get milk from . . . peaches,' said a deep, warm voice. Sally felt her peaches turn to red as she turned to see Mr Matthew Tregonna grinning at her. Her grip tightened on the baby, causing her to squirm uncomfortably and turn her head from side to side. 'Which one is that?' he said.

'Baby Joiner. Nurse Cary is examining Mrs Joiner. She was having a lot of discomfort while she fed the baby. I had no idea that it could cause so much trouble.' It was easy to hide her face behind the baby, making a pretence to put her to her shoulder to bring up more wind. It was easy to talk of patients, babies and maternity, but impossible to meet his gaze. *He's laughing at me. He considers me fool of the month, to be teased and insulted whenever he meets me.* She walked to the closed curtains. 'Mr Tregonna is here, Nurse Cary,' she said, distinctly.

'Oh, good . . . can he come?'

'Mr Tregonna, could you see Mrs Joiner?' said Sally, and held the curtain slightly aside for him to go to the bedside. 'If you'd wait for just a minute, I'll get a mask,' she said, and handed the baby to another nurse. She had the satisfaction of seeing Matthew Tregonna wait while she brought a fresh mask for him to put on before attending to a woman just delivered. He put it on and washed his hands thoroughly at the sink near the cubicle. Sally again held the curtain and glimpsed the turned-back sheets and the blood stain on the bed. She took the baby again and wondered if she should put her back in the nursery. It was only day one when there would be little milk for her before the flow began in earnest on the third day.

'Where's the baby?' said Matthew Tregonna.

'Oh, you're as bad as Sister. It hurts, I tell you,' grumbled Mrs Joiner.

'And I expect that Sister told you the same as I've just told you, that every time the baby sucks, it makes your womb contract and stops any oozing of blood from inside. It's better medicine than giving you drugs. Nature still knows best sometimes.' Sally was amazed at his gentleness and patience and Mrs Joiner seemed to lap up his flattery when he told her that she was a very lucky woman to be so healthy and have such beautiful babies. 'We'll give you something this time, but let the baby suck for ten more minutes and Nurse will give you something to help it contract.' He took Myra Joiner's hand and placed it on her flabby abdomen. 'Now hold that . . . like that. That's right. Can you feel a lump down there?' She nodded. 'Not a very hard lump as yet. Hold the baby to suck, Nurse Ashford. Now, what is happening to it?'

'Ouch, it hurts and it's getting harder.'

'And the oozing of blood is stopping. It's clamping down on all those tiny blood vessels and stopping them from bleeding.'

'So it is . . . I shall be able to feel it when I think I'm getting damp, down below, and be able to tell Nurse. Sister told me about it, but I've never felt it for myself, Doctor.' Myra Joiner beamed and held the baby. 'You're ever so nice, all of you.'

'Glad some people think so,' said Mr Tregonna. He left the cubicle and Sally fetched a clean draw sheet and a back tray to clean up the bed and make Mrs Joiner comfortable. When she came back, the doctor had gone and the ward seemed empty without his taut, strong figure with the untidy hair and now tired blue eyes.

'He hasn't been to bed yet. He had to see a new admission—query Caesarian, query induction. I told him I'd call him if there was any sign of her going into labour or if the baby was having trouble. She's a high blood pressure and needs to have that baby soon.'

'Is there anything I can do, Nurse. Feeds are finished and beds made. There aren't any more treatments on the list in the office. 'She looked at the bed patients who were showing signs of feeling the oppressive heat.

'Yes, you can come back to Pre-natal and keep an eye on the new one. She needs cooling down, but she's on restricted fluids due to her blood pressure so we can't fill her up with iced water . . . and, of course, she might have to have an anaesthetic, which means nothing by mouth for several hours before the operation. I wonder, I know it's a bit old fashioned in hospitals such as Beatties, but a cooling sponge is good in some cases.'

'We did them in PTS, but apart from a case of very high temperature with a patient having a malaria rigor, I've never done one. I do remember the details. Sponge one limb at a time and let the beads of water dry naturally, then cover it and sponge another, taking the temperature and in her case, her blood pressure, after each limb.'

'That's right, and you know you have to stop if the temperature drops a degree as it will drop further even without more sponging.'

Sally nodded. 'I might ask her to move over. I feel hot and sticky.'

'But less red in the face now that our Matthew has gone.'

Sally blushed again. 'He thinks I'm a fool and a little scrubber.' Nurse Cary laughed. 'I seem to have a talent for letting him find me at a disadvantage. First when I told him off over the stethoscope, then in the nurses' home when Dorian Warner was fooling around and I landed upside down in an armchair, and now when I was cooing over the Joiner baby when she burped.'

'Ignore him. I think he's great, but he can be a little arrogant.'

'A little? I'm not used to such rudeness.'

'He was worried yesterday. You have to make allowances for that on this ward. Everything can be calm one minute and hectic the next.' A bell rang. 'What am I saying? That's the side ward.'

Nurse Cary hurried away and Sally cleared the clinical room and put the soiled linen in the sluice room, ready to be counted and put down the laundry shute. The bell in the side ward rang again and Sally went to answer it. Nurse Cary met her at the door. 'It's Mrs Trevor! She says she feels twinges. Get the trolley, will you?'

Sally hurried away for the trolley, quickly checking that everything was there. So Mr High-and-Mighty Tregonna hadn't taken any equipment this time!

Lucy Trevor was whitefaced and obviously very frightened. She clutched at Nurse Cary's hand when she placed the foetal stethoscope on her tense abdomen to listen to the heart beat of the new life waiting to be born. Sally held her hand and spoke gently, telling her that everything was going to be all right, and gradually the worried expression subsided and the young woman sank back and let Cary listen.

'Fine,' said Nurse Cary, briskly. 'Now tell me where the twinges start and how long they last.' In five minutes the picture was clear. Mrs Trevor was in the very first stages of labour, with many hours before she could expect to be delivered. 'I think you ought to have a nap,' said Nurse Cary. 'A rest now will leave you fresh for your delivery,' she added, kindly.

'I'm frightened,' said Mrs Trevor.

'Of course you are. You've lost the others and now you are going to have a live, healthy baby, if we can possibly manage it.' Mrs Trevor closed her eyes in resignation, as if she couldn't believe what she was told, but expected a repetition of her earlier misfortunes. Nurse Cary whispered the dose of the relaxant that she wanted to give the patient and Sally hurried away to prepare it. In half an hour, Mrs Trevor was asleep, with a tired smile on her face. Cary patted the bed. 'Pray God we make it,' she murmured.

'Was the foetus all right?'

'Very good. If she has it now, it will be only three weeks premature. I'd better alert the labour ward in case of accidents.' Nurse Cary checked the notes for blood group and case history and nodded. 'I'll ask Nurse Bastable to sit with her when she comes on duty. They've masses of staff in babies' and they'll have to thin out this afternoon during the lecture. Is she reliable? I haven't met her yet. Sister had her under her wing for a couple of days and then I was off duty. I've seen her and the patients seem to like her, but she hasn't been in here yet, has she?'

'Nurse Bastable is very efficient. I heard that she won a silver medal for surgical nursing in her training school. She'll soon pick up the routine here. After all, I'm a stranger here, too, but it all slots in to routine I recall from my training school.'

By lunch time, Violet Bastable was firmly established by the bed in the side ward, watching the sleeping woman and noting the times of the very faint contractions. 'Who is going to deliver her?' she asked, knowing that at a certain stage in their training, pupil midwives and the medical students taking the same course, took names of admissions and tried to follow them through all the stages of labour to delivery.

'Not you, Nurse. You'll do all your deliveries in the Redlake. You do most of the theory here and the quota of deliveries in Surrey. The nurses in the labour ward have been to Surrey and are doing their practical here. I think that you are the lucky ones. You have Sister Beringer to teach you here and the labour ward in Surrey is well equipped, even if it isn't as up-to-date as Beatties. However, you will be watching when there is time to spare and you can be free of ward duties and lectures. If something unique comes in, I advise you to stay even in your off duty. Some conditions are seen so rarely that you might miss the one and only opportunity.'

'And a registrar or consultant is on call at all times?'

'Of course. I hope that Mr Dillinger is back as Mr Tregonna must be very tired after last night and today.'

Sally went to lunch and was told to collect the dispensary which was needed to replace drugs used during the night and likely to be needed again soon. The pace was fast in the wards and the labour ward was busy with both tables occupied with normal deliveries. The lay-out of the complex was well

designed to shield the pre-natal patients from the
sights and sounds of the labour ward which so often
seemed alarming when they were nothing of the
kind. Each department, for comfort, cleanliness
and hygiene, was separated from the others, if only
by a short corridor or thick door.

Mr Dillinger came and went, leaving a trail of
untidy beds behind him and examining two patients
before the busy nurses even knew that he was in the
ward. Sally decided that he was good. He spoke to
the women in a soft, Southern American voice, and
his eyes held a twinkle of humour. The patients
responded to his calm and unhurried presence and
even Sandra White made an effort to sit up and look
attentive when he explained what she could expect
when she went into labour. 'Why are you here?' he
asked her. 'You are perfectly well and I would say
that you aren't due for at least another two weeks.'

'The doctor said I could come in and have it
taken,' she said. 'He spoke to the social worker
about it and she told him about the place where I
live not being suitable. Wish you'd all hurry up. She
said that if I'm out of here by next week, there's a
vacancy in a home where I can stay for a while until
they take the baby for adoption.'

'But we don't induce babies, that is, bring them
on at a given time, just to meet a time table.' Mr
Dillinger looked annoyed. 'I can't think which doctor had you admitted.' He turned to Nurse Cary.
'Do you know about this, Nurse?'

'I was told that Mrs White was Dr Warner's case,
Sir.' She took a deep breath. 'I wanted to talk to

Sister about it, but there hasn't been time. Can you tell me where Dr Warner fits into the unit, Sir?' She reddened, slightly.

'I think we'd better talk in the office,' he said, and Sally could hear nothing of what passed between them, but as he passed her in the ward on his way to the labour ward, she saw that his mouth was set in an angry line.

'Nurse Ashford!' Staff midwife Cary walked quickly back from seeing the consultant to the door. 'I now know the picture. Dr Warner hasn't the authority of Mr Tregonna, who is our senior registrar. He has no authority over the nursing staff and any doubts you may have about anything he might want to do in the ward must be told to Sister, me or the registrar. Mr Dillinger hinted that Dr Warner wants to do many things that this hospital never does—like this routine induction of labour to get deliveries over at a time convenient to the staff. Sandra White is a case like that. He was in out-patients and thought that as she had no real home and nowhere to take the baby, she would agree to this method.' She shrugged. 'It would fit in with the social services who like to have times and dates and can plan where to send people like Sandra. I think that Mr Dillinger will be talking to Dorian Warner, but if he asks you to set up for an interuterine drip, check with someone first.'

'I will, Nurse Cary. There *are* cases when the method is used, to the advantage of the patient, would you say?'

'Yes, if we want to get a baby out because the

mother or baby are showing signs of distress, of course it's good, and many lives are saved by this method, but to risk infection by introducing a . . . what amounts to a foreign substance, into the body just to speed things up for perfectly healthy women who should *enjoy* having their babies, is unnecessary and in some opinions, unethical.'

'Can they ever enjoy having a baby?'

'Oh, yes, if they've done their homework and learned to relax properly and everything goes well, they say that the actual birth is a peak of joy and fulfilment. I've seen several women in tears of joy, not tears because of pain.'

'May I go to the lecture, Nurse?'

'Goodness, is that the time? Yes, Sister will tell me off if I keep you here. She hates unpunctuality.'

'I can guess,' said Sally, with a smile. In the main corridor, she saw several doctors striding to their several departments. All looked busy and oblivious of anything not concerned with the business of healing. A man with a tall, rangy figure and untidy hair loomed up against the bright sunlight and Sally almost suffocated with the thought that it was Mr Matthew Tregonna. Why get into a panic if you think you've seen a button on his coat, she thought. Am I a nurse or a cringing little mouse? But it wasn't fear of his sarcasm that made her feel like a first-day probationer nurse each time she saw him or saw someone resembling him. It was an emotion that she had never had with this intensity.

A boy on the beach with rippling muscles and a wide, white smile had moved her when she watched him surfing, and he had come to her with drops of water dripping from his hair. That had been a hint of what physical attraction could do, but it had no comparison with this charged sensation that mingled reluctant admiration for a perfectly proportioned body, a fine, strong face that told the world he would suffer no fools lightly and the subtle effect that even his displeasure had on her heart. Men like him can reduce a woman to nothing . . . to a limp and pathetic bundle of compliance, she thought, resentfully. He thinks you're an idiot and you know that you could never get together even for a brief affair.

Sally ran the last few yards to the lecture room. It would be bad enough to be late for any reason, but far worse if she was late because she daydreamed about the man with blue eyes who haunted her thoughts in such a disquieting way.

'You seem amused, Nurse Ashford. Perhaps you can tell us the first signs of labour.' Sister Beringer pounced as soon as Sally entered the already full lecture room. 'Come on, Nurse. We haven't all day.'

CHAPTER FOUR

'I'LL have to go home next weekend,' said Nurse Sally Ashford glumly. 'Sister Beringer is giving us so many notes to write up that after this one long weekend I shall have no time to go to Bristol. If I don't go soon, they will all think I'm dead or kidnapped.' She smoothed out a wrinkle in the towel on which she lay, sunbathing on the roof of the hospital. 'Last night, first my mother rang to see if I was all right, then Brian rang saying that he would be coming up here to see me if I didn't go down this weekend.'

'Why this weekend?'

'I said ages ago that I had this time off, long before I thought I'd want to stay here.'

'Well, he is your boyfriend, isn't he?'

'In a way, more from habit than anything like a burning passion.' Sally took off her sunglasses to let the sun reach her eyes so that she wouldn't have white rings instead of an all-over gentle golden brown tan. She tried to visualise Brian, and Charlotte had asked her to describe him. 'He's good-looking, if you like fair men,' said Sally, not seeing any connection between the very blonde Brian and the deeply golden hair of Matthew Tregonna.

'Blue eyes?' Charlotte was smiling. 'You seem to go for blue-eyed men.'

'I don't!'

'I'll let that pass,' said Charlotte, blandly. 'What does he do? He sounds rather nice.'

'He's a biology teacher in a large comprehensive school. Very good, at it, or so I heard. He plays sports and keeps fit and . . . that's about all.'

'That's not what I would call about all. He sounds nice and solid and reliable. Just the type to make a good husband.'

'Oh, don't you start. You sound like my mother. She's quite dewy-eyed about him and drops hints as subtle as bricks every time she sees us together. Heaven knows what she says to him when I'm away, but he seems to take it for granted that one day I will come to heel like a good little pet dog.' Sally sat up to rub sun-tan cream into her arms. 'I'd ask you to put some on my back, but you are in no fit state to sit up,' she said. Charlotte lay on her front with her bikini top undone so that the line of brown wouldn't be marred. 'It's so hot, but isn't it good to have a tan at the beginning of the summer! I shan't have to wear tights for months except on duty.'

'You can't reach.' The tube of cream was taken from Sally's hand and the grinning face of Dorian Warner came very close to hers.

'Get lost,' she said, trying to grab the sun cream.

'Ah . . . temper,' he said, holding it just out of reach.

'Do you mind? Oh, what's the use. Keep it.' Sally lay down on the towel. 'I'll just lie here and fry.'

Dorian unscrewed the top of the tube and squeezed cream on to his fingers. 'Don't bother,' said Sally, a little ashamed of her outburst on seeing him. After all, she did want her back creamed and the sensation of long, slender fingers gently circling her bare skin was soothing and very pleasant. In spite of her distrust, she couldn't deny that he was physically very attractive and that his touch, now that he was caressingly gentle, was very good, sending tiny waves of pleasure over her back. 'Thank you,' she murmured. 'That will do very nicely.'

'I'll do your front, too, no trouble at all,' he said. She gave him a dirty look. 'All right, but a guy has to take his pleasures when he can get them in this hard world. Do you know that I am on duty for the whole of the weekend, with Mr Dillinger waiting in the wings? I can't leave the hospital except to go as far as the Falcon where they can reach me by telephone, I can't go to the baths—too far they say—and I can't find anyone to share my lonely vigil.'

'My heart bleeds for you,' said Charlotte. She moved uncomfortably, unable to find the ends of her bikini and feeling vulnerable with a man like Dorian Warner staring at the line of her bosom on the towel on which she lay. Sally saw her predicament and did up the straps. Charlotte sat up to face the smiling man. 'I suppose you'll tell every night nurse how lonely you are and how misjudged you have been at Beatties.'

'Think they'll believe me? When do you come on nights?'

'Not until we go down to Redlake Hospital for the second half of our six months midwifery.'

'Not as popular with staff, I gather. I was talking to a nurse in the labour ward who said she was glad to be back at this hospital.'

The shadows grew long and dark between the chimneys and Sally began to gather her belongings together. Dorian watched her and she wished that the bikini was less revealing. It was strange that the same minute pieces of silky material worn in a public swimming bath or on a crowded beach were quite acceptable, but on the roof of Beatties, with just one man watching her and Charlotte, she felt naked. Another man appeared in the doorway that led to the stairs down to the corridor. Sally gasped and had an almost panic-stricken desire to cover herself with her rather gritty towel.

Matthew Tregonna hesitated and then walked towards the small group. He nodded curtly to Dorian. 'They said you might be here. There's been another admission. I am off duty this evening and going away tomorrow. I'd like to examine the patient with you before we come to any decision about her.' He looked at the girls and his gaze flickered over the golden limbs of the girl with the deep chestnut hair. He watched her toss back her hair and wondered why she looked so sad. 'Sorry to break it up, but we ought to see her,' he said. He turned away without speaking to either girl.

'See what I mean,' said Sally, trying to sound lightly indignant. 'Very rude, very self-opinionated and totally devoid of *savoir faire*.'

'Poor man was embarrassed by the sight of all that luscious flesh,' said Dorian.

'After working on the midwifery block?'

'Different . . . very different,' he said, and walked away with a lazy wave to them. 'Be good, until you see me again,' he called.

'Did you have any luck with a lift?' said Charlotte as she put a cotton skirt over her bikini and added a tee shirt. She waited while Sally did the same. 'We can go into supper like this, can't be bothered to change again.'

They walked down to the dining room. 'I can't see a note for the journey down, but I did put my initials by one for the journey back. Someone left a car number and said they'd be at the Clifton end of the Suspension Bridge at eleven a.m. on Monday morning. I wonder who it is. They must be going from here in the first place to have put the note on the board.'

'They may have a car full for the journey down,' said Charlotte. 'Someone may be going for a longer break. Can you remember the car number? I know a lot of cars as I've been here for centuries.'

After queueing for salad and cold beef, Sally opened her bag and found the note she had made of the car number. Charlotte frowned. 'Never seen this one. It must be a new member of staff or someone has changed their car. It's not new, by the registration number. Four years old or more. It could be someone from the unit as there is a congress in Bristol at the moment about paediatrics. Might be the rather nice man on children's ward.

Not that it would do you any good. He's married. Married a nurse here last year.'

'I'm not looking for romance—I only want a lift,' said Sally, plaintively.

'Nice to combine the two,' said Charlotte. 'I put my name on the board for next week. If it means taking Dorian home for the weekend, I don't care. He would at least give the village something to talk about.'

'You warned me about putting a name but you are doing just that! And with Dorian on the loose!'

Charlotte smiled, complacently. 'I shall be in the position that he will have to ask me if he can drive me home. I can give a fair performance of the unwilling girl and then grudgingly ask him to stay and take me to a charity cabaret for which I *happen* to have tickets. It will let me off one particular hook. My mother had a partner all lined up for me. He gets a little warm in this weather—reminiscent of the horses he rides and the other company he keeps. Believe me, in that company, Dorian would appear to be almost normal.'

'Well, I ought to pack. I'm catching the coach from Victoria at ten, so I shall come to early breakfast as if I was on duty. I want to know if Mrs Trevor has her baby before I leave. I know it isn't a good idea to carry ward worries away with me, but she's so sweet and patient, even if she gets a bit up-tight at times, poor girl. Who wouldn't after all she's been through?'

'You could pop up to the ward and wait outside.

I'll slip in and see if she's been delivered. See you at breakfast.'

The dawn light through the poplars promised another fine day. What had made her wake with such a start? Sally looked out of the window, leaning out so that she could see at least a part of the drive leading to the main hospital entrance. The air was cool and full of early summer as the scent of late blossom came up to her window from a rogue pear tree that had just happened to grow from a seed dropped by a bird, or a passing nurse eating a pear—who could tell—but the froth of blossom gave a hint of a bumper harvest of fruit for whoever got to it first. An ambulance drove slowly out through the wide-open gateway and Sally thought that the doors slamming had caused her to wake early, but as she leaned out, dressed in her brief, cool, baby-doll pyjamas, she heard voices, and the smell of tobacco mingled with the scent of flowers. Two men were talking as they walked slowly past her window. Sally drew back, conscious of her flimsy attire.

'You know that you must call Mr Dillinger at the slightest hint of anything wrong? I shall be miles away and, this time, I intend staying for a whole weekend.' The voice was flat and grim, as if the speaker had endured as much as he could take from the man at his side.

'You go now. It will be OK, I tell you. I'm not a complete idiot,' said Dorian Warner, resentfully.

Matthew Tregonna shifted the soft leather suitcase to his other hand. 'I could stay on a bit, but I think if I do I shall never get away. I should have gone last night, but the Caesar had to be done.'

'You're right, of course. I'm sorry if I was less than efficient, but I didn't think the infant was all that distressed.'

'Cord twice round her neck and hardly any viable placenta?' Matthew Tregonna gave a short laugh. 'Just as well we got her straight to the theatre. However, that's what midder is all about. Near panic and then a beautiful baby and a mother who has forgotten all her fears a few hours after delivery. Just take it all slowly and check everything. Check everything yourself even if it sounds like a false alarm. Babies don't wait for consultations, or had you noticed?'

'Have a good weekend, and thanks a lot. I'll concentrate on getting my quota of normal deliveries done and leave the clever stuff to more experienced hands.'

'If you learned that tonight, you learned a lot. Good . . . I think that's my taxi. See you.'

Sally peeped from behind the net curtaining at the tall man striding down the drive to the waiting taxi. He was wearing a pale blue shirt of silk and light-weight biscuit coloured trousers. Sally wondered how a man who looked so tired could still appear so handsome and have such a buoyant step. He's going away to his family, his parents or . . . his wife? Something in his walk made her certain that he was longing to get away to someone who was longing to see him. She dressed quickly, filled with

a sadness that she could not define. Matthew Tregonna was looking forward to his weekend off, even
though he was so dedicated to his work and would
be anxious to know the progress of some of the
"ladies in waiting" on the midwifery block. Why am
I so reluctant to go home? I have a family and Brian
waiting for me. I should be eager to see them all
again. I have lots to tell them and they will have
news, too.

Where was he going? She knew so little about
him, apart from the fact that he despised her,
thought of her as a cheap joke, a girl who let people
like Dorian Warner kiss her and who seemed to do
the wrong thing every time he saw her. Did he live
within a taxi ride of Beatties? Did he have to catch a
train or was he going by air to somewhere like the
Scilly Isles or Paris, or Scotland now that the
weather was good?

Sally snapped shut the lock of her case and
caught up her velvet jacket. She shut her room door
and went over to the dining room for breakfast.

'Hello, you look very holidayish,' said Charlotte.
'Wish I was off, too.'

'I'll come up to the ward when you go. I think
they must have had a Caesar last night.'

'You come in here all dressed up and tell me that.
They didn't call you, you lucky thing?'

'No chance. I was dressing and Dorian and Mr
Tregonna went by the window talking. I listened,
quite unashamedly.'

'And they looked up and saw a vision in those
very sexy pyjamas that you wear?'

'Good grief, no! I was wondering what woke me up and I looked out to see if anything was happening up by the main gate. Then I heard voices near, and bobbed back. I'm sure that they didn't see me . . .' she said, no longer quite so sure. They were walking slowly and she hadn't noticed them for a minute at least while she was leaning out of the window. 'No, they didn't see me. Dorian would have whistled or made some coarse remark,' she said, as if to convince herself.

'So Mr Tregonna had to stay on. That must have upset his plans. I thought he was off for the weekend.'

'He is. He was on his way down to a taxi. He said he was to have gone last night but could still make it. I wonder if he had far to go.'

'He was going by air, or so I heard.'

Sally crumbled a piece of bread and no longer felt hungry. So he was leaving the country for the weekend. There was no way that she would see him during the next two days. She tried to laugh at herself. As if she would have seen him at any time even if he was only five miles away. One look at me and he'd be ten miles in the other direction, she thought ruefully, and wondered what made it important to her. I don't like him, he's rude and cruel to make fun of me in front of other people and we could never have anything in common.

'You're catching a fairly early coach. Come on, we'll get up to the ward before I'm officially on duty and I can tell you the news,' said Charlotte.

'Right. I'll leave my case in the lodge and ask

Claud to call me a taxi.'

The smell of fresh antiseptics and cleanliness greeted the two nurses as they walked up to the ward. Sally sat on the bench outside feeling alien, like a visitor, in ordinary clothes. Charlotte was gone for five or ten minutes, but it seemed like an age. The door opened and Charlotte came back, smiling. 'Your favourite patient had a lovely little girl last night. Mrs Trevor is still very tired, but absolutely over the moon. Her husband has been in to see her and they both had a good cry together.' Charlotte beamed. 'Good old Beatties. She's best at this sort of thing. That baby could have gone the way of the others, but now the Trevors have a healthy live baby to fill their lives.'

Sally began to walk away. 'What about the Caesar?' she asked. 'Anyone I know?'

'You saw her in ante-natal, but she wasn't due until next month. Off you go before Sister gives you a job to do.'

Sally walked out into the sunshine, with a feeling of thankfulness. It wasn't good to let work flow over into her off duty and usually it was easy to avoid, but the sight of the woman's face had haunted her and she knew that she would have thought about the Trevors and worried while she was away. Now, I can put the hospital and every one in it out of my mind, she thought. She turned firmly to the gate and chatted to Claud while she waited for the taxi, avoiding giving direct answers to his many nosy questions. Instead, she filled in the time asking about the people in authority at the hospital. It was amusing to hear how much he knew and to realise how important it was, as Charlotte had told her, to keep personal matters to herself where the porter was concerned.

'I expect most of the senior staff are married,' Sally said innocently.

'Did you have anyone in mind, Nurse?' said Claud with a leer.

'No . . . Mr Dillinger is, I believe, and some of the sisters have married doctors and stayed on in different departments, haven't they?'

'Oh, yes, we have lots of doctors marrying nurses. People like that new one, Dr Warner, come and go . . . they never get fixed up, although it isn't for want of trying. Others have girl friends away from the place—take that Mr Tregonna. He must have someone stashed away, won't never say anything,' said Claud in a wounded tone.

So, Matthew Tregonna and I have that in common, at least, thought Sally. 'Which one is he?' she asked.

'Tall, fair haired . . . you must know him on midwifery. Went off like the clappers this morning to the airport. Must be meeting someone or he wouldn't have been in such a hurry; but if he had a plane to catch . . . he had to catch it.'

He doesn't know if Mr Tregonna has a girl friend or not. The thought filled her with a lightness that made her give Claud a dazzling smile. 'Thanks for getting me the taxi . . . I think that's it now.' So if Claud hadn't found out the chances were that Matthew Tregonna was not married or engaged.

Not that it matters to me, she told herself, but I just wondered what sort of a woman could put up with his sarcasm.

It was pleasant to be driven down the motorway, past the green fields and soft hills of Surrey, west to the higher ridges and orchards. The bushes that had grown on the cut edges of the embankments to the roads cut through the undulating countryside. Even the concrete bridges had a certain grace as they framed pictures of landscapes and farmyards. Sally watched cattle grazing quietly in fields close to the busy roads and recalled reading that when railways were in their infancy, cows would run away at the first sight or sound of any vehicle that was not horse drawn. Now, the cows hardly bothered to look up at the constant flow of brightly coloured metal and glass that flashed by at high speeds.

As London was left far behind, she was poised between her two worlds. London has seemed so real, so substantial only an hour or so back in time, and now the hills were becoming more familiar, the signs on the high gantrys told her of places she had visited from her home in Bristol. She dozed in a shaft of warm sunlight and opened her eyes to see a sign pointing to Bath, another to Chipping Sodbury and to Doddington. Nearly there, she thought, and wondered if she could afford another taxi from the bus station. I'll see if there's a long queue for the bus first and if there's a bus due I can take that. Brian would collect her, and so would her father if either was available. With a slightly guilty sensation she hoped that neither had waited around hoping for her to telephone. It would be good to get back to the house with no fuss, to go to her room and change her clothes before she had to make conversation.

Do I have to prepare myself to meet people I love? Have I changed so much in such a short time that I can no longer come home casually, to take up the threads again without bracing myself? They can't have changed. Any change will be in me, any strain in meeting again will be of my doing. The line of people waiting moved up as the single-deck bus arrived at the stop. Brian will expect me to be the same. She couldn't remember if they kissed each time they met. If we do, it will prove that we have been apart and have to make a definite sign that we are together again . . . and if we kiss like people in love, it will make him believe even more that we are a pair, made for each other as he and my parents believe.

Sally dragged her case from the bus and walked along the road to the small development of houses beyond the wood. The trees were densely leafed, with swaying clouds of light green above her, full of bird song. She relaxed. It was the same, only more beautiful, with early summer in full bloom. The fact that the house was on the outskirts of the city gave the area a feeling of being in the country and she longed to walk in the woods near her home again. She quickened her steps, glad to be nearly home. She might have changed in her outlook to work and have grown away from the city she knew so well, but surely she would be pleased to see Brian again?

Her key turned in the lock and a flurry of fur hurled itself at her. 'Rastus!' she said, and bent to bury her face in the rough fur of the rangy dog that seemed to think she had been away to the moon. Well, the first welcome was all that she could want. The door to the sitting-room opened and her mother was there, calling to her father that Sally was home. The last doubts as to her need and love for her home left her. 'It will be all right,' she whispered to the dog. 'It will be all right with Brian, too.'

The garden was colourful with border plants and blossom. Trees sighed in the woods with a different sound from the high poplars of Beatties and somewhere, another dog barked, making Rastus race to the wall at the end of the garden. Sally sat in a garden chair and answered questions with good humour, then announced that she was going to put the kettle on and who wanted coffee? She slipped back into the family routine and was glad that her father just grunted "Tea" as she went back to the house, instead of them treating her as a guest.

'Brian rang,' said her mother. 'He's coming round to see if you've arrived. Said something about going out this evening,' she said, vaguely.

'What if I have a date already?' said Sally.

'Go on, you haven't. You can't do that when you haven't seen him for such a long time.'

Sally smiled, but once more was conscious of a gap between the girl who had trained in Bristol and gone about with Brian as loving friends, and the girl who had begun her work in London and met men like Dorian Warner who wanted her sexually and made no secret of the fact . . . and Matthew Tregonna, who filled her heart with such a turmoil of emotion, of dislike and shyness, of anger and the dawning of an emotion never felt before, of physical awareness that threatened her composure each time she saw the back of his white coat as he walked the corridors of the teaching hospital.

Brian would take her for granted as he had done for years. He was good and honest, a fine athlete and a caring friend. Did she want him as a lover or a husband, to vow to love till death do us part? Was her feeling for him the love that could shatter convention or make her feel like a goddess when he touched her? She picked up a book of poems while she listened for the kettle to whistle. It fell open at a page at which she had smiled indulgently when she was only a few months younger, but which now seemed to leap out of the page at her in letters of flame. It was a poem by Rupert Brooke, the man who had died so young in the first world war, died while his heart was young and torn with desire for love and for his country. Sally had read his descriptive poetry and loved it, but this was something more . . . something that had seemed over emotional until now. She read it as if for the first time.

. . . What can I give you as a token,
A sign that we have met at last?

I'll break and forge the stars anew,

Shatter the heavens with a song;
Immortal in my love for you,
Because I love you, very strong.

Your mouth shall mock the old and wise,
Your laugh shall fill the world with flame,
I'll write upon the shrinking skies
The scarlet splendour of your name,

Till Heaven cracks . . .

Sally stared at a bird that sat on the edge of the bird
bath splashing water over its feathers. She closed
the book and switched off the kettle. It was impossible. Just because she read a piece of poetry
that stirred her untried depths it didn't mean that
she was in love with the moody man from Beatties.
A shiver that was half ecstasy went up her spine . . .
desire was something that had no part in her re-
lationship with Brian. Occasionally, when they
kissed, she felt a growing awareness of him and
found the experience enjoyable, but this feeling, of
which she knew so little, was more like a disease
than a gentle diversion. 'I don't like him,' she said
as she poured water into the pot. 'I don't even like
him.'

But as she walked across the lawn with the tray, it
was Matthew Tregonna's mocking mouth she saw
in the shadows, not the surprised smile of Brian
who waved to her from a garden chair.

CHAPTER FIVE

THE salad had been crisp and delicious. Sally took another dollop of cream and covered the fragrant strawberries. 'You spoil me,' she said. 'Any food other than this would be impossible today, but it's so delicious that I shall put on pounds.'

Her mother smiled. 'Pity that Brian couldn't stay for lunch. What time are you going out tonight?'

Sally frowned and took time to pick out a perfectly shaped berry. 'He said he'd call here at six.' Her mother went into the house to make coffee and Sally finished her meal. Brian had been so pleased to see her that she wished she could have responded more enthusiastically, instead of being glad of the presence of one delighted, energetic dog that wanted her attention at the same time.

'What will you do?' he had said. 'I wish I could cancel the match, but you know how it is, Sal.'

'I know, don't worry about it, Brian. I shall be glad to laze here, or I might take Rastus for a long walk.'

He bent to kiss her cheek. 'I knew you'd understand. We'll make up for it this evening. Fancy a concert?' She shook her head. 'No, perhaps not. It would be too hot tonight.'

'What's Rachel doing?' Sally wondered suddenly if Brian's sister, with whom she had been at school and liked as a friend, might be available to go with them wherever they decided to spend the evening.

'Oh, she's away in the Midlands. She finished her teacher training and hoped to get a job near to her old college. Can't think why she wants to go so far away. I trained here and hope to live here for a very long time.'

'Haven't you ever thought it would be good to see fresh faces . . . new places? You went to school here and, apart from a few holidays, I don't remember a time when you put a foot out of Avon.'

'Suits me . . . just one thing missing now that you have deserted us.' He grinned. 'Hurry up and finish that stupid course and come home where you belong.'

'You think I belong here? Why here and not London, Brian?' Sally regarded him with large, sad eyes. 'Since I went to Beatties, I don't know where I belong.'

'You should never have gone,' he said, brusquely. 'Admit it . . . you made a mistake and now you regret it. You've wasted your time, the hospital's time and my time, with all this nonsense.'

She looked at him in silence, shocked to see how deeply he was affected by her absence. She looked at her wrist watch. 'Isn't it nearly time for the match? I should hate to waste your time any further.'

'Oh, Hell! . . . I didn't mean that, Sal. Look. I have to go, but I'll come for you at six and we'll go for a meal somewhere and a long talk.'

Sally smiled faintly. 'See you later, if the boys can bear to let you go.'

He bent to kiss the tip of her nose. 'Be good,' he said.

Sally wandered back into the house with the coffee tray and washed the cups and jugs, her hands acting mechanically. When she had stacked everything away she had no knowledge of what she had done, apart from registering the fact that this must be the second time that day she had washed up, once after Brian had left before lunch, and now, when the meal was over and her mother had gone to the kitchen garden to gather more strawberries to be used in her favourite recipe for strawberry shortcake.

If only Brian would accept the fact that there was no future for them together. Sally looked out at the dazzling sunshine. I wonder if I've been fair to him, she thought. I've said I didn't want to be married for ages, at least until I finish midder, but I haven't sent him away with no hope of my changing my mind. The thin shirt was sticking to her back. She thought longingly of the sea, or if that was impossible, of a good, cool swimming pool.

'I think I'll go to the Baths, if you don't want the Mini,' she said as her mother emerged flushed and slightly dusty from the kitchen garden.

'I don't know what to do with all the fruit. Can you take some back with you?' She saw the car keys in Sally's hand. 'Car?' she said, vaguely. 'Yes, that's all right. I don't need it today. Going somewhere? I thought you were going out with Brian.'

'Not until later. He said he'd call for me at six, but you know how it is with him. If they win, they'll stop for a drink and it will be seven before he gets home.'

'I think he'll be on time. You've no idea how much he's missed you, Sally. I wish you'd never gone to that place.' She hesitated and her face set in a defiant expression. 'I try not to say anything, but I think you should have stayed and got married.'

'I know you do, but it's my life, Mum, and I want to see a bit more of other places and meet other people before I settle down.' How could she say that she had met a man who could make her weak with annoyance and longing? How could she convey the fact, either to Brian or to her mother, that a man who despised her and found her faintly ridiculous was the only man she could love? I don't like him, I have twenty thumbs when he's around and he does nothing for my concentration on my work, and yet I can't get him out of my mind. 'I could do some shopping, if you want anything,' she said.

'We could do with more fresh cream and icing sugar. Oh yes, better get some eggs and I'll make some crème caramel.'

'Right . . . no, don't bother to get any money. I'll settle when I get back.' Sally smiled. The sure way of changing any subject that became embarrassing was to switch her mother's interest to cooking. 'I'll pick up my swimming things and be back by five.'

'See that you are,' called her mother. 'You can't keep a nice man like Brian waiting for ever, you know.' Sally turned down the corners of her mouth and went up to her room. It really was on everybody's mind. Ah, well, a good brisk swim, a shampoo and a walk with Rastus might give her the poise she needed to handle Brian.

The roads were fairly busy with cars taking families for picnics on the Downs. The sudden, early heat wave had brought out old cars that had been laid up all the winter and mopeds that sounded as if they needed a spring clean and overhaul. Sally wondered if some of them had even passed their annual test for reliability. She was glad she had her student's card with her, together with the book of tickets she had been given by Brian for when she wanted to use the university swimming pool. Even with the university up in term time, the tickets would make sure that she was granted admittance.

The small reception desk was littered with piles of shampoo sachets and small combs, reminding swimmers to buy if they had forgotten to bring either item. Sally bought a shampoo and went up the stone steps to the changing rooms. She quickly changed into a leopard-print bikini which she had never worn. It was a present from a cousin with a warped sense of humour, who had sent it with the message: "Me Tarzan, you Jane", which was guaranteed to make her reluctant to put it on, but as it was the only one she had in Bristol, she had no choice. I shall meet strangers and who cares what they think, she thought. She tugged at the bra to make it fit and a glance in the mirror showed that it was even more revealing than she had imagined.

She glanced at two girls who were leaving the

shower that had to be used before entering the
swimming bath and took courage. They were very
well endowed and wore very brief snippets of bright
nylon and good suntans. If they feel confident, why
should I worry? thought Sally. She walked sedately
down the steps into the deep end, luxuriating in the
creeping coolness of the water. There were few
people in the bath and she sat on the bottom step
waiting for a gap in the swimmers before slipping
into the water and swimming two lengths, using a
fast crawl. She shook the water from her hair and
brushed the droplets from her eyes. 'Sorry,' she
said, as a girl bumped into her.

'Great, isn't it?' The other mermaid grinned.
'Don't mind me, I could bump into someone in an
empty pool.' It was one of the girls who had gone
through the shower. 'Like your bikini . . . this thing
was cheap. It pays to have a good one.' Sally
glanced down at the half-exposed breasts. At least
her top gave the support of a well-cut bra while the
one the girl was wearing sagged and did nothing for
her full figure. 'But you look great in it—I wish I
had your figure,' the girl continued.

'This is the first time I've worn it. I thought it a bit
brief.'

'If I looked like that, I'd buy one like it, but not
when I went out with Sam . . . he's bad enough
when I'm wearing a high-necked sweater.'

She swam away, leaving Sally uncomfortably certain that she too would not want a boy friend to be
near her when she was wearing anything like this.
She climbed the steps and sat on the edge of the

pool, but a group of men came laughing through the shower and she was too self conscious to stay out of the water. She slid down the side of the pool and felt a tug at the back of her bra. The men were walking along the edge of the pool, past the spectator stand and the tiled mural on the wall. The tallest man climbed to the highest diving board and looked down into the water. His friend shouted to him to go in, taunting him and saying he was chicken. The man grinned, lifted his arms and took the pose of an Olympic diver.

Sally gasped. Olympian indeed. The broad shoulders rippled with latent strength, the deep chest, covered with enough fair hair to make a haze of gold, rose as he took a deep breath. The taut sinews of the stomach flattened and the muscles of the long, gently tanned legs tensed. He tossed back a lock of deep gold hair in a remembered gesture and Matthew Tregonna took the air in a graceful curve, splitting the water with the minimum splash and nearly touching bottom.

Sally took a long, shuddering breath. It was not altogether because she was surprised to see him there, in Bristol, in the university pool, but because she knew that when she slid into the water, the small, inadequate catch on the single width of ribbon used to secure her bra had come apart, and the tiny garment had floated away. She swam after it in feverish haste. She could see the soft material floating just under the water, but sinking fast like a small ray fish. She dived and saw, through eyes that were stinging from the chlorinated water, another shape much larger than her bikini coming up from the bottom of the pool, making straight for her. She tried to avoid a collision and gulped water. Coughing and nearly blinded, she was forced to the surface by the impact of the two bodies meeting under water.

'What the hell do you think you are?' The hair was dripping over the furious face as the angry man held her arm firmly, while he patted her none too gently on the back, aware only of the fact that he had collided roughly with a stupid girl who was now coughing like mad and must be kept above the water at all costs. His general attitude gave the impression that he was dealing with a rather imbecilic child who needed help but who was a nuisance. Sally struggled and tried to break away. 'Stop that,' he said. 'Have a good cough and I'll get you to the side.' To hold her more firmly, he put an arm round her shoulders and held her closer. 'Lift your head . . . do you want to inhale more water? Put your hands down.'

Sally saw her bra lying soggily on the bright blue bottom of the pool. She kept her hands firmly over her chest and wriggled away, treading water. 'Christ!' she heard him say as she dived deeply to retrieve her lost garment, and a moment later, he came down like a shark following a dolphin, his shadow dark beside her. A quick thrust of his long legs and he got there first, picked up the trophy and swam upwards, gathering her under his arm as he passed her and bringing her to the surface. He was laughing as he shook the water from his face, but

Sally had no spirit left to notice the humour—the gentle humour in his eyes. She grabbed the bra and turned away, putting it in place over her heaving bosom. She felt his hands at the back, taking the ends and fixing them back into the clasp, and had to stay still while he did so. For a second, his hands pressed her shoulders as if to reassure her.

'It's all right,' he said. 'Don't worry. I'm the only one who noticed.' He turned her to face him and she knew that he recognised her as she swept the wet hair from her face.

'Thank you,' she said in a whisper.

'You? In Bristol?' His expression changed and a darker look came to his laughing eyes. He pushed her to the rail and dropped his hold on her as if she was suddenly red hot. His gaze travelled from her face over her body down to her feet that floated slim and childlike in the clear water. He saw the troubled flush under the drops of water that hung like tears on her cheeks, and the growing shame in the fearful glance she gave before she stumbled from the pool and ran for the changing room. He lay on his back on the water and looked up at the decorated ceiling. 'Holy godfathers,' he said.

Sally grabbed her towel and rubbed her hair, then realised that she would smell of chlorine if she didn't wash her hair. She found the sachet and went back to the hot shower, turned on the spray and stood under it, rubbing the soft and fragrant lather into her hair and down her body.

As she wrapped herself in her towel she thought wryly, at least he can't come in here! Why him? Why should he be here at the same time as she was? she asked herself for the tenth time.

She smiled, ruefully. It must have been as much of a shock for him to see her as it was for her to see who was holding her with such impersonal, but gentle, care. Had he missed his plane . . . perhaps from Lulsgate Airport on the outskirts of Bristol? He could have flown from London to Bristol and be staying with friends. She put the required coins in the hair dryer and sat on a tall stool, combing her fast drying hair and trying to dismiss Matthew Tregonna from her thoughts. I have to meet Brian tonight and I mustn't spoil his evening. I have to go back as if nothing had happened. But how could she ignore the memory of those hands . . . those strong, firm hands that held her up in the water safely while she coughed out the water she had taken in when she dived? The hands that had thrust her away to the safety of the rail as soon as he knew who he was holding; who he was almost caressing in the cool water. He couldn't get rid of me quickly enough, I'm not exactly deformed! she thought, resentfully, and as anger took over from her embarrassment, she firmly packed her towel into the plastic bag and flicked the ends of her hair over the top of her tee shirt, feeling cool and fragrant and, in spite of her encounter with Matthew Tregonna, restored.

'Did you have a good swim? I almost wished I'd gone with you, and, I must say, you look cooler.'

'I wish you *had* come,' said Sally. 'I nearly lost the

top of that ridiculous bikini that Sue sent me. You can put it out for the next jumble sale. It's a menace.' Her mother chuckled. 'Good job there weren't many in the pool,' said Sally.

'You should have gone with Brian,' laughed her mother.

'Not in that thing. I'll never wear it again. I think I'll go back to regulation black swimming costumes like I wore at school.' She held it up between two fingers. 'Look at it. I was mad to use it, but I haven't another here.'

'What did Sue say when she gave it to you? Guaranteed to break the ice at any swimming pool?'

'Guaranteed to do all kinds of damage,' murmured Sally. As for breaking the ice, it had the opposite effect. As soon as Matthew Tregonna had seen who she was, his amused, slightly flirtatious air had dropped from him like a discarded cloak leaving a barrier of ice between them, a thick impenetrable barrier through which they would never touch again, mentally or physically. 'I'll get changed in case Brian comes on time.'

It was still very hot and Sally looked through her wardrobe, finding half-forgotten dresses from last year, summer jeans and faded tops. He hadn't said where they would go and Brian might as easily have booked a table in a smart restaurant as be prepared to take her to a jazz club, a Clifton pub or a hamburger bar. She selected a cotton skirt of soft green with hazy mauve flowers on the print border and topped it with a silky green shirt without sleeves.

She found high heeled sandals and put them on her glowing tanned feet, making a mental note to take some flatties in the car in case they walked on the Downs. A light shirt would do as a cover if the evening grew cooler or if the midges began to devour her.

'You look very pretty,' said her mother, accusingly. 'I hope you know what you're doing.'

'I'm not doing anything but go out with an old friend.'

'You be careful. It's all very well to go out with him and make him think there's no-one in the world like you, but if you don't want him for keeps, it's time you said so.'

'But I've never said I'd marry him, Mum.'

'He thinks you have, or he expects it—same thing.'

'No it isn't. I haven't promised anything and I don't want to get married to Brian or . . . anyone.' Her mother looked at her sharply and Sally had the uncomfortable feeling that she saw more than appeared on the surface. 'I'll try not to hurt him,' she said gently, and went to answer the door bell.

'You see! On the dot, punctual.'

Sally looked at her watch. 'One minute early, in fact,' she said, and smiled.

Brian took her hand and tried to pull her towards him. 'You look wonderful . . . and you smell nice, too.'

She drew away. 'It isn't Chanel Number 5. It's that rather overscented shampoo they sell at the baths. You never did have any nose for quality,' she said, trying to keep the conversation light.

He glanced at her feet. 'At last you trust me to take you somewhere that doesn't require training shoes or hill walking boots.' He grinned. 'The lads are meeting at the Volunteer.' He saw the growing horror in her eyes. 'It's all right. We *did* win, but I said I had a very important engagement tonight. I've booked a meal on the boat.'

'What boat? Don't tell me you've taken up sailing?'

'The restaurant in the docks. Don't you get any news from home? They've anchored two boats and have food and music on board . . . very lush and just the place for two people on a warm evening.'

Sally tried to smile, but was aware of the light in his eyes and knew that her absence in London had done nothing to make him forget her. Dear Brian, she thought. I do love you . . . I could have loved you before . . . What happened to people who never met a man who was like a torrent of unease, a hurricane of emotion sweeping through their lives, even if it left devastation in its wake? What happened to them? Were they as she had been before going to London? Happy in simple pleasures, less compelling urges, happy to marry someone of whom they were fond, like Brian? 'Let's go. I can't wait to smell the river,' she said.

'It isn't smelly any more. In fact, if someone falls in the water now, they don't make them have a stomach washout! It's getting better all the time and fish are coming back up-stream.'

'Well, don't expect me to eat any fish caught in

the harbour.' They laughed and argued happily as they drove to the docks. If it could be like this all the time, perhaps I could be happy, and make him happy too, she thought, and as they walked across the cobblestones by the huge warehouses, she was content to let things ride and hoped that Brian would do so too. Giant cranes leaned over the water like prehistoric monsters waiting to grab their prey. Boats of all kinds lay at moorings and a swan with young swam soundlessly across the channel. 'The swans seem quite happy,' said Sally, 'but I can't believe there are fish here.'

'You have to admit it lacks a certain something.'

'The smell?'

'The smell. Remember it when we walked along the tow path further down the river? the day we took Rastus and he fell in the mud?' They laughed and were silent as they looked across the glinting water towards the towering bulk of the *Great Britain*, the iron ship that had come home to her beginnings as the first of her kind, to the rest of Brunel's best, within sight of his graceful suspension bridge. Brian brought drinks out on to the deck and they watched small boats going home. 'We had good times,' he said, quietly. Sally glanced at him and saw that there was suffering in his eyes.

'Yes, we had good times,' she said, slowly. She knew no elation, no relief, even though she now knew that he had given up hope of winning her. 'We can still have good times,' she said.

'Yes, I hope so, but you've changed, Sal. I knew it as you walked across the lawn this morning and I knew it more clearly when I saw you tonight. Who is he?' He turned to face her, his eyes hard.

'He . . . there is no man in my life, Brian.'

'If I didn't love you so much, I might believe you, but I know every change of mood . . . or I did before you went away. You have a certain bloom that I can't describe or account for, something in your eyes that tells me you are someone's woman.'

'That's not true. I haven't been out with anyone at Beatties. I've worked hard, and being away from home, I suppose I've had to depend on my own inner resources, but I haven't a boy friend there.' And never will, she thought. 'Nothing has changed, just my work and wider interests. I even play darts now!' She saw him relax. 'Don't look so incredulous. I play in the bar of our local, a nice pub where all the Beatties people go. I'm really quite good,' she boasted.

'Perhaps we should have joined the lads after all,' he said, and led the way to the restaurant.

'This is good,' said Sally. 'How clever you are to find this place.' He looked at her with a wry grin. 'I love the water, it makes me feel peaceful,' she said.

'I was banking on it. When I booked this meal, I had an idea that we would eat and take our time talking about . . . things.' Sally looked down and crumbled her bread roll. 'I missed you so much, Sally, and I hoped that when you went away you would look back and know the worth of the things and people you left behind you.'

'It's good to be back,' she said with sincerity. 'I love this city.'

'But not enough to give up your course and come back to live here?' She shook her head. 'I had it all planned, but I suppose that makes me the original chauvinist . . . to hope for a wife to be there when I come home and to have her attention exclusively mine.'

'You're very sweet, Brian. I do love you, but not like that, not now, while I have something to offer and something to gain from living away from here. If I settled down, I would be looking back and wondering what I had missed. That's no basis for happiness, even with someone as good as you.'

Brian looked into his wine glass as if he had just seen the wine and wondered how it had got there, although he had tasted it and approved it ten minutes earlier. 'I love you, Sally. I don't know what's happening, but something or someone has come between us. I feel it and see it in every gesture you make. Who is he?'

'I told you, there is no other man who takes me out,' she said. 'Can't you see that it is the sense of freedom that makes this difference? I am independent now, with all the good and bad times to manage on my own without running home in my off duty. I've had to make more friends and to explore strange places, to meet different sets of people. I need time to live this through. I can't come back now.'

The lights of the city shimmered across the water and the silhouettes of the old warehouses stood sentinel to the evening dusk. A light breeze brought relief from the heat and Brian smiled. 'All right.

We'll forget that for a while. It's enough to have you here and to have this evening.' He was more serious than she had known him and her heart ached to make him happy, but in spite of her real affection for this man who had known her for so long and had shared her growing up, she couldn't put out a hand and tell him she loved him. The music from the disco along the quay came faint and muted, a background of sound for the words that ran through her head . . . more from her favourite poet, who must have suffered strange passions to have written,

'Ah! not now, when desire burns, and the winds call, and the suns of spring
Lightfoot dance in the woods, whisper of life, woo me to wayfaring;
Ah! not now should you come, when the road beckons, and good friends call,
Where are songs to be sung, fights to be fought, yea! and the best of all,
Love, on myriad lips fairer than yours, kisses you could not give . . .'

Kisses you could not give. Sally turned misty eyes to the ripples of silver under the lamp light and heard the sounds of the city and her heart cried for other lips . . . that were stern or tender, but never unexciting, and never for her.

CHAPTER SIX

RASTUS barked as if he knew that he was in luck. Sally glanced out of the window and saw her parents get out of the family car and her mother walk warily over the gravel in her new and rather tight shoes. Lunch was cooking and there was at least an hour before it would be ready.

'You should have come,' her mother said. 'We had a new man today who made even your father listen to the sermon.'

'But I *did* prepare the food,' said Sally, self-righteously.

'Several people asked after you and at least two wanted to know when you were getting married.'

'Big deal,' murmured Sally. That was one of her reasons for avoiding the Sunday morning gathering outside the friendly little church to which her parents went each week. 'I'll take Rastus on the Downs for a run,' she said. 'Be back in time for lunch. I left the timer on and the sauce is covered with film.'

Rastus danced away to sit by the car, knowing with uncanny instinct that Sally would take him in the big car. She slid behind the steering wheel and glanced back to make sure that the big dog was lying on the back seat and not standing up looking out of the back window. 'Good boy,' she said and drove slowly to the end of the driveway. In five minutes, the Downs opened before her, the vast expanse of green and trees made beautiful by far-seeing Victorians who had also taken the precaution of setting the area aside for recreation for the people for ever. It was evident that the sun brought out everyone who had some form of conveyance, and that the beautiful slopes near the Suspension Bridge were a meeting place for people to enjoy the views over the Avon Gorge. Rastus ran wildly over the green grass, still fresh this early in the year, and almost untrodden after a wet spring. The scents of new growth came sharply up to mingle with the last of the May blossom and from the river below came the whistle of a train entering the tunnel by the Portway.

Sally called to the dog and he came more sedately to walk along the path overlooking the Gorge. She rested one hand lightly on the shaggy head and lingered at the look-out point towards the slender string of metal that was the bridge, slung between two towers of warm stone and metal. As always, she was struck by the grandeur of the deep gorge and her lips twitched with amusement as she overheard a woman trying to tell her son how the deep ravine had been made. He seemed bored at the geological details and Sally couldn't help feeling that he would remember Bristol more easily if he was told the myth about the formation of the gorge, where the giant Gorham had scooped it out of the earth together with his brother Vincent. Gorham had rested from his labours sitting in a place still called Gorham's chair, in the woods at Blaise, while Vin-

cent was turned to stone and became the rock called
Vincent's rock by the side of the gorge.

Couples walked by the hedge, close and holding
hands. Sally stroked the dog's head and tried to
think how lucky she was to be there in the sun with
the animal she loved. It was all so beautiful, but she
knew it was not the place for her on her own . . . it
was a place for lovers. She saw a girl with bright hair
gazing up at her man. He bent to kiss her lips and it
seemed natural to do so in such a setting. They
walked close together down the slope and Sally
turned back, calling sharply as Rastus had disappeared. It only needs a bitch in season to come
across his line of scent, she thought with near panic.
Rastus had spent many nights away from home
patiently pursuing various loves. She breathed a
sigh of relief. A man on a bench was holding the dog
by the collar and trying to read the identity med-
allion on his collar. Rastus was panting gently, with
his pink tongue lolling and his eyes bright.

'Thank you,' said Sally. 'I lost sight of him for a
minute. I don't think he'd wander far up here, but
there are so many trees and bushes it's easy to . . .'

'Well, well,' said a deep, amused voice. 'Are you
in the habit of losing something every day?' She
blushed scarlet. 'First she loses valuable hospital
equipment, then her dignity in the kitchen of the
nurses' home. Yesterday . . . now what did she lose
yesterday?' His eyes were insolent and full of
laughter. 'Can you recall what you lost?' His hand
still held firmly to the dog's collar and Rastus edged
away from Sally as if he thought she would put him

back on a leash when she caught him. 'And today, one big rough hairy animal.' He ruffled the hair behind the dog's ears. 'Friendly animal, but dogs do like me,' he said, complacently.

'That dog is a fool,' Sally said, coldly. 'He doesn't know the difference between a friend or a . . . tramp. He would kill a burglar by licking him to death with pure affection.'

'Well, he's met someone in yet another category. I'm not a friend, I suppose, at least not from the look of that terrifying scowl you're wearing. I didn't think I was a tramp . . . would you know anything about tramps, I wonder?' His glance took in the slim lines of the summer dress and Sally was conscious that in the interests of coolness, she had not worn a waist slip, and remembered how the light shining from behind her must show every line of her thighs under the flimsy material of the skirt. She stood sideways and looked out over the gorge.

'When you've finished with him, I'd like to take him home,' she said, stiffly.

'We're just becoming acquainted,' he said.

'I'm sorry, but my family are expecting me for lunch.'

'But you don't live far away, five minutes by car, or can I give you a lift?' She looked at him sharply. 'Oh, yes, I had time to read the tag. Good boy, Rastus,' he said, and the wretched traitor of a dog snuggled up to him adoringly, making tiny sounds of pleasure as his ears were rubbed.

'I have a car,' said Sally. 'Come, Rastus.' The dog looked at her sadly. 'Come on, you lazy dog,' she said, trying to sound as if she had some control over him. The strong brown hand held the collar. 'Will you please leave him to me,' she said.

'What a pity.' He rose from the seat and still held the dog. 'Just as we were getting to know each other.' Sally couldn't tell if he was talking about the dog or about her.

'I must go.' She turned away and called the dog and to her relief he followed her at a slow amble. She walked with a straight back, hoping that she wouldn't trip over the rough ground that was the shorter way to the car. She reached the clump of bushes by the old Camera Obscura and glanced back. 'Oh, *no*!' The dog wasn't following. She hesitated and saw Matthew Tregonna walking slowly towards her with Rastus prancing at his heels as if he had known the man all his life.

'Seems that he isn't as hungry as you are,' said the man with the disturbing eyes. 'He likes me. Now what do they say? Love me, love my dog . . . or is it the other way round?'

'It doesn't follow.' Sally tried to smile naturally. 'Thank you for catching him again.'

'No trouble. He seemed to think you'd forgotten to take me too. Came to fetch me, didn't you, Rastus?'

'I'll put him on the lead if you'll hold him for a moment. The car's over there.' Matthew Tregonna looked at the line of cars. 'That's it, now behave, you naughty dog,' said Sally, jerking the lead slightly.

'I'll walk with you to the car. You're parked quite

close to me. Did you drive down?'

'No, this is the family car. I came by coach.'

'When do you go back to London?'

'On Monday, bright and early. I have a lift back,' said Sally.

'Pity. I have plenty of room in mine.' He handed her the end of the lead as she stopped by the car and his fingers touched her hand. She looked up, conscious of the wave of sensual awareness that his touch provoked, and could read nothing in his impassive eyes.

'Thank you again,' she said. The couple who had kissed came down to sit on the grass. The young man dropped the bag he was carrying and took the girl in his arms. Sally unlocked the car and thrust Rastus into the back seat, slamming the door after him. She avoided looking at the couple on the grass, but as she turned, Matthew Tregonna was close behind her and she swayed to keep her balance. They touched and his hands pulled her closer, his lips hard on her mouth. Dizzily, she tried to push him away, but her hands fluttered as useless butterflies and her legs seemed lost in a crumbling pit of sand. She fought the desire to return his kiss, but her mouth was soft and mobile under his, the lips parting and sharing the long moment of ecstasy. Trembling, she groped for the car door, dragged at the door handle and sank into the passenger seat.

He looked down with a sardonic smile. 'You're a little reluctant to give thanks where thanks are due, so I took it . . . and it seemed a thing to do.' He nodded towards the couple on the grass. 'We must come for a . . . picnic the next time we're here.' He strode away without a backward look and unlocked his own estate car about fifty yards away. Sally eased herself over to the driver's seat and looked in the rear-view mirror. She was sure she had never seen his car before, but the numberplate seemed familiar. She combed her hair and applied fresh lipstick and wondered why she looked so normal, so happy, when the only emotion she ought to feel was anger, and humiliation.

She sounded the horn as soon as she drove the car into the garage. Rastus leaped out and ran to the house as if he had been away for months and couldn't wait to see the family. He greeted Brian with enthusiasm and Sally remembered that he was invited to Sunday lunch. 'He was a very bad dog,' she said. The large creature seemed to laugh at her. 'Yes, very bad,' she said, severely. 'A man caught him and I put Rastus on the lead.'

Brian's glance was searching. 'It doesn't seem to have worried you. You have more colour in your cheeks than when you came down yesterday. Did he try to pick you up?'

'Who?'

'How many were there, for crying out? Did you lose the dog all over the Downs? The man who stopped him, of course.'

'I suppose he did, in a way.' She saw Brian's jaw harden. 'But I can handle men like that quite easily,' she said, with more conviction that she possessed. Who would be capable of keeping a man like Matthew Tregonna under control if he really wanted anything? She took the dog's lead into the house and went to wash before lunch. No wonder Brian wondered what had happened, she thought, seeing the sparkle in her eyes as she saw her reflection in the bathroom mirror. 'I hate Matthew Tregonna,' she told the smiling girl in the mirror. 'I hate him and I know that he was only being his normal, forceful, objectionable self, making his arrogant presence felt.'

'Are you going to be all day?' called her mother. Sally smoothed down the skirt of her dress over the waist slip she had put on and demurely went to the patio where the table was laid. I'll put him out of my mind, she thought. I shall be free of him until I go back to Beatties, and when we are in a working atmosphere, he will be his usual conceited, rude self . . . and easy to dislike.

It was easy to sit in the sun and make light general conversation with her family and Brian, who seemed to have lost the hurt expression and was enjoying the fine weather and her company. Sally brought out sun loungers and even the battered sunshade that hadn't seen the light of day for a couple of years, as the weather had been generally windy whenever the sun shone during the past two summers and not hot enough to justify the effort of putting it up when the weather was calm.

'Do you think this will last for weeks and weeks?' she said as she settled down to read the Sunday papers beside Brian who lay full length on a rug on the lawn. He glanced up at her face, shadowed by the sun shade, and admired the line of her leg along the side of the lounger. 'I love the sun. I think when I've finished midwifery, I'll get a job abroad in the sun.'

'It's one thing to laze about and drink cool fruit juice all day, but you'd find it trying to work in the heat.'

'Oh, you . . . always the practical soul without any imagination,' she said, lazily.

'And you'll get freckles if you stay in the sun,' he said, complacently. 'You always did and you always will.'

'Heaven protect me from the man who grew up with me,' she said, and refused to go with him for a walk. 'I've had enough walking, especially with that dog.'

'Oh, I don't know.' He turned over and propped his chin on his hands. 'You looked very . . . bright when you came back. I wondered if I could work the same magic. Who did you meet this morning, Sal?' His voice was quiet.

'I told you.'

'For a simple attempted pick-up he made a great impression. Either that or you have a face in your mind that makes you go all dreamy, even during lunch.'

Sally blushed. 'Rubbish,' she said. 'If anyone looked dreamy at lunch it was you. I've never seen such drooling over my mother's strawberry short-cake. I thought that you were on the verge of running off with her!'

'Could do worse, at least she'd talk about you all day and feed me well.' He reached up to take her hand and she let it rest in his. The same sensation of warmth existed between them and his maleness added a dimension that was satisfying and flattering, but there was no danger, no conflict, no desire in the touch. 'Must you go back tomorrow?' he said.

'Yes. In a way, I seem to have been here for ages, but I do know what you mean. This is very pleasant.'

'And when you forget about us, as you will as soon as your coach leaves the bus station, what do we do then?'

'I'm not going by coach, I'm getting a lift.'

Brian sat up. 'Who's taking you?'

'I don't know.' She laughed and told him about the scheme at Beatties where names or car numbers were put on the list of people offering or wanting lifts. 'So you see, it might be the Matron, it might be the mortuary attendant or all ranks in between.'

'Or some conceited lout wanting a quick thrill.'

Sally eased herself into a semi-reclining position and glared. 'There aren't men like that at Beatties. If that happened just once, the whole scheme would have been dropped ages ago.' But she remembered the naked passion of Dorian Warner when he forced that one kiss on her lips. I hope that Charlie knows what she's doing if she rides with Dorian, she thought.

'What about the man who answered the phone when I rang you at the nurses' home? He sounded pretty high handed. Very much the God-substitute-consultant.'

'Oh, that was Mr Tregonna. He wouldn't use the scheme. Only the friendly sort willing to help out would do that. He isn't the type.'

'So he's as bad as he sounded.'

'He's a good doctor, but he doesn't like taking messages for all and sundry—nor do I. It gets a bit much when you expect a call and while you wait you answer the telephone for half a dozen others who all seem to live two floors away.'

'Well, at least he brought you to the phone.' Brian dismissed Mr Tregonna from his mind and sank back again with the sun on his face.

'It isn't going to last.' Mrs Ashford put the radio down by the lounger. The area weather forecast was coming after the general forecast. They listened to a chilling tale of thunder storms breaking up the heat-wave from the west. Sally looked up at the cloudless blue sky. 'They said in the general forecast that by tomorrow the whole country would be cooler, with rain in most parts.'

'It will last until I get back. So, all the more reason for making the most of this,' said Sally. 'I know some people who will be glad to have it cooler.'

'Come on, snap out of it, Sal. Nearly lost you again. Stop thinking of those women in labour. You can't do anything about them and you told me yourself that it was bad discipline for nurses to think or talk shop in their off duty.'

'How right you are, sir,' she mocked. 'I promise to forget them so thoroughly that when I get back I shall have to learn their names again.' She closed her eyes to the sun and relaxed. The heat shone red through her eyelids. It was like a screen on which images flitted and wavered. She saw a stern face looking at her from a man who wore a stethoscope round his neck. She saw the same face in chilling contempt as he watched her legs waving in the air from the chair into which she had fallen when Dorian kissed her . . . the face relaxed into a devilish glee as the water of the swimming pool opened up and showed the naked top of the diving girl . . . and . . . she opened her eyes wide, refusing to see him again, with a dark deep look of something to which she could put no name, but was mixed with desire and sadness.

'You were asleep.'

'Just thinking.'

'Do you always snore when you think?'

'I was awake. I heard Mother calling the dog and the front-door bell.'

'So, you missed the visitors.'

'Someone important? I didn't hear anyone come out in the garden.'

'Just your neighbour to borrow the hose. Your father hasn't stopped muttering that he won't see it back until next autumn. It's enough to make it rain.

'And now the telephone. I have to go, Sal, so I'll answer it on my way out. See you at dawn or whenever it is we arranged. I thought it was to take you to the station, but the Bridge will be better.' He sprinted across the lawn and Sally admired the athletic build and the strength of his stride. If only we had that spark that is more than the awareness of two young creatures together . . . if only . . .

The telephone stopped ringing and Sally wondered if he had reached it in time to answer it, but
she was much too comfortable to move. If he didn't
get there, they'll ring again, and it wouldn't be for
me, as hardly anyone knows that I'm at home. She
heard Brian's car start after five minutes and her
mother called her to fetch a tray of tea.

Sally wrapped the tie-on skirt over her shorts and
went into the house. 'Who was that?' she asked,
with no real curiosity. 'Did Brian get it in time?'

'Yes. I was in the kitchen garden and couldn't get
there, so I was glad he was here.'

'So, was it Mrs Thing next door hinting that they
could do with half a ton of fruit?'

'No, it was for you, didn't Brian fetch you?'

'I was in the garden. He went to answer it and
said he'd see me in the morning. He's taking me to
the Bridge where I pick up my lift.' She frowned.
'Are you sure? He didn't call or even wave from the
doorway.'

'He went off looking very put-out, I thought. He
said it was someone you knew but he had handled
it.' Mrs Ashford paused. 'No, that's not what he
said. He said, "I fixed him . . ." yes, that's what he
said.'

Sally couldn't think who would telephone her at
home. If it was the hospital, they would have said
and Brian would have told her mother. Who knew
that she was coming home? From Beatties there
were only Charlie and Dorian and she couldn't
imagine Dorian ringing her. A bird in the hand was

his policy and he wouldn't waste a good Sunday afternoon languishing over a girl he could pursue when she returned to London. It was a man, her mother said. Her face cleared. Mrs Ashford had told her that a woman at church was heavily pregnant and that her husband was a bundle of frayed nerves, frightened that she would start in labour before he got her home. 'It might be Hazel's husband. She wrote to me and said that I was well out of the way in London now that the baby was due. Her husband wanted to call me in to look at her the last time I was at home, so now the time is nearly here he will be even more anxious about her.'

'But surely Brian would have called you?'

Sally laughed. 'Brian has a thing about me having my brains picked when on holiday. I never really mind unless they get too intrusive, but he gets hopping mad if he thinks I'm being used when there are G.P.s and nurses being paid to give them the information needed. That's it, for sure. Brian gave him a few crisp pieces of his mind and rang off. Poor man, do you think I should ring back?'

'Leave it. By now he will be on the line to his doctor, which he should have done in the first place. Now, take this tin of cakes . . . they get so dry if we put them on plates in the garden.'

'Mother! You can't expect us to eat another crumb!'

'There isn't much for supper and you know you like fruit cake.' Her mother smiled. 'You must take some with you for whoever is giving you the lift . . . in fact it would be polite and rather nice if you took a picnic.' She went back to fetch the sandwiches. A picnic . . . Sally recalled the man and the girl on the Downs with the picnic bag forgotten as they lay in a close embrace on the cool grass. A picnic . . . Matthew Tregonna had laughed at the thought. She could hear again the laughter, feel the fingers digging into her back and the tilt of her head as he forced it back for that one soul-shattering kiss. She put the tray down, shakily. This was terrible. What if she recalled the incident while doing something important in the ward? When would they go to Redlake Hospital? Time was passing quickly and it would be sooner than most of the girls in her set would like it to be. But not for me, thought Sally. I wish I was going straight there instead of having the possibility of facing that man again. He may be on holiday—no, he had told her he was going back the next day, had offered her a lift. She breathed deeply. It was providential that she could say with honesty that she already had a lift and didn't need his offer.

'Come on, if you cut some sandwiches, we can store them in a plastic box in the fridge. Take that half bottle of wine and some orange squash and some fruit and cake.'

'Whoops! That's enough. I'm not supplying a full bus load, although I suppose there may be several of us in the car.'

The air was cooler as the evening came and Sally helped to pick the fresh crop of ripe strawberries when the sun was gone from the plants. She packed them carefully, thinking that the girls in her set would enjoy them with ice-cream. She found herself wanting to get back to the friends she had made in such a short time. She packed her clothes and added more summer dresses in case she needed them in London, bathed, and lingered in the cool garden, walking and talking with her father until bed time and the lonely hoot of an owl.

A car horn made her run to the front of the house early the next morning. She looked at her watch and saw that it was at least half an hour before Brian was due to collect her. She couldn't see his car through the thick flowering shrubs, but saw a tall form lounging on the wall. I suppose he has to get to work and realised that he would be late if he took me at the agreed time, she thought, and hurried into the kitchen to gather up her luggage. She heard her father talking and saw that he had taken everything but the food, which was still in the fridge. Sally gathered it together and packed it in the large insulating box with the wine and other drinks. 'Goodbye,' she called up the stairs to her mother who was still in bed, and heard her muffled reply.

'Change of plan, I see,' said her father as he kissed her in the doorway.

'A bit early. He's probably in a hurry. I'd better go.'

'Nice guy . . . you must give us a ring and say how you got on.'

'What are you talking about, Dad? I know he's a nice guy.' She ran down the path and pulled the gate behind her so that Rastus wouldn't follow. She bent to pick up the box again and found a hand already there to take it. She looked up and went cold. 'You? What does this mean? I was expecting someone to take me to my lift.'

'It seemed a pity to tie up two chauffeurs in one morning, as I was taking you back to London, anyhow,' said Matthew Tregonna with a slight, enigmatic smile. He opened the car door and Sally got in, hardly knowing what she was doing. 'Don't look at me as if I'm abducting you. You have the car number you were to look for?' She fumbled in her bag. He told her the number of his car and she knew why it had seemed familiar the day on the Downs. She nodded, dumbly. 'I'm sorry you hadn't time for fond farewells, but I know that your father will get in touch before he leaves home. Nice guy, your father.'

'But how did you know I was your passenger?' said Sally, her colour returning.

'I rang yesterday to say I'd call for you instead of you bothering to go out to the Bridge.'

'And Brian answered it?' It began to make sense.

'A very cross masculine voice told me to go to Hell and that he was taking the day off to get you back to town.' Matthew negotiated the traffic at the roundabout and smoothly joined the commuter run through the city.

'But he'll be expecting me. Let me out, take me back . . .'

'Now we don't want an accident, do we? Calm down, Sally, and listen. Your fiancé seemed to think that I was some kind of threat to him. I tried to assure him that my intentions are fairly honourable . . .' he smiled. 'I've seldom heard such nasty suspicions. Interesting, but lurid.'

'What do you mean? He isn't my fiancé, he's someone I've known all my life.'

'Who is in love with you and sure that he will marry you. Come off it, Sally Ashford, who do you think you're deceiving?'

'Me?' She sank back, deflated. 'How you have the nerve to ignore what Brian said and practically abduct me half an hour before he was due to pick me up, even after he told you that you wouldn't be taking me back to London, leaves me speechless.'

'Good,' he said, calmly. 'I like to drive in silence until we leave the city behind. There are plenty of fools on the road all late for their offices and not driving with due care.' He drove well and Sally was aware of the control he had over the powerful car. Control over everything, she thought. Control over his own life, his promising career . . . his emotions?

They drove through the Cotswolds and away from the London motorway. Briefly, he apologised for making the journey longer than the straight run to London.

'You should have left me to Brian,' was all she said, ungraciously. 'I shall be in the way.'

He ignored her remark and smiled in an irritating, superior manner. 'We can stop to eat somewhere,' he said.

'You can leave me in the car. I've brought my own food,' she said, rudely.

'Enough for an army . . . and I've already been

invited to share. I had quite a chat with your father, who assured me that you had stayed up till the small hours preparing goodies for my delectation.' He drove down a side road that led to a canal bank which was a favourite spot for fishing and picnics, but on a week-day out of the holiday season was verdant and deserted. He parked in the shade of a tall elder bush and took the insulated box which he placed on the car rug spread in a cosy dip by the bank. 'Wine? So I even have Bacchus on my side,' he said.

Sally glowered at him, her heart thumping madly. It looked heavenly out there on the rug by the softly flowing stream with the man who scared her and obsessed her. 'Come on,' he said, gently. 'This place was made for . . . picnics.'

Sally slowly joined him, trying to avoid all physical contact, putting out the food carefully as if she had to impress an important visitor, as she kneeled on the rug.

'You look like a Geisha girl about to serve tea,' he mocked, and accepted a glass of wine with his food. And what happens to the Geisha after the party? thought Sally. What happens after the picnic?

CHAPTER SEVEN

'I THOUGHT I saw you when I came out of the nursery, Nurse Ashford,' said Lucy Trevor. 'You didn't know I'd had my baby, did you?' She looked at Sally with a hint of reproach in her clear eyes.

'Ah, but I did. I came up to the ward to see if you had been delivered and I know that you had a lovely little girl. I couldn't go away before I knew what was happening, could I?'

'Did you really? Did you come up here?' Mrs Trevor blushed with pleasure. 'But I might have known; everyone here has been so kind and interested, it's like having my own family around. Sister let me walk back with Nurse to see Baby tucked in.' She smiled. 'She's the prettiest baby in the whole nursery.'

'I'm sure she is,' said Sally. 'Look, I'll pop in while you feed her next time, but I have to go now. I've been in orbit ever since I came on duty.' She turned away to the clinical room to clear the trolley and to set up again for an internal examination.

'Did you have a good weekend?' called Violet Bastable. 'See you tonight and we can have a nice chat.' They passed each other quickly and Sally wondered how such a peaceful ward could suddenly erupt into this hectic scene, with two new admissions who had both left it rather late to come in, without giving the unit any warning, and who looked as if they were racing to get to the labour ward first. Two husbands were kicking their heels in the outer waiting room, ready to take wives and babies home, and Sister was busy telling the new mothers details of the individual diet sheets that she had made out to suit the requirements of each baby. Two other husbands, waiting to hear news of the mothers-to-be, were looking tired and worried, to the slightly superior amusement of the men whose wives were safely delivered. How soon they forget that they were just as worried only a few days ago, thought Sally, as she looked in to tell one of the men that his wife was ready and would he take the baby.

She could hear the voice of Dorian Warner coming from the corridor leading to the labour ward. He sounded angry and the woman's voice answering him was cross, too. She glanced back and saw Charlotte, looking both apprehensive and defiant, but there wasn't time to find out just what was happening. She saw that the bed occupied by Sandra White was made up ready to receive her back from the labour ward, with the bedclothes loose so that the patient could be put into bed easily. The Caesarian-section lady was sitting up in bed, reading and looking very well, the puffy bags under her eyes gone as soon as the baby was born and the effects of her high blood pressure had subsided.

'I'm really back!' said Sally.

'Did you doubt it, with all this waiting for you?' Staff Nurse Cary grinned. 'Seems like you never went away, doesn't it? Well, I can tell you, we could have done with your help and we certainly needed Mr Tregonna last night when the emergency prem. was born.'

'Don't tell me that Sandra had a prem.? I thought she was nearly full term but admitted because she had housing difficulties.'

'No, this was one brought in by taxi from a cinema. The poor taxi driver was *very* worried. Didn't fancy himself as a midwife.'

'Who delivered it?'

'I did, but the baby needed a bit of help and our Dorian was busy with his blasted drip.' She saw that Sally was puzzled. 'Oh, you didn't know, did you? He admitted Sandra with the idea of inducing her by interuterine drip and because his boss was less than enthusiastic, he started it when Mr Dillinger had left for home.'

'Has she had the baby?'

'Not yet . . . stupid man hasn't done one before and he's all talk and no experience to my way of thinking. He had no right to start it without permission, and when Sister rang Mr Dillinger, I thought the telephone would catch fire! Of course, Dorian can't take the blame. Oh, no, he tried to say that Charlotte hadn't left the right equipment on the trolley for him, and he hadn't even asked her to lay it up last night. He just took a sterile dressing trolley and some drips and bungled it.'

'Is that why Charlie looks upset. They seemed to be having quite a row outside the nursery.'

'Is he here? Just let me get my hands on him,' and

Nurse Cary fled, looking like an avenging angel. '*Now* do you think Beatties doesn't produce the best men? I don't know where Warner trained, but it must have been in the bush,' she called as she reached the door.

Gradually, the tempo slackened and the ward returned to normal. The mothers for discharge had gone, with many fervent vows of gratitude and "I'll never forget you all", at which Sister Beringer smiled diplomatically, knowing that once the family returned home, they might be slightly less grateful after a series of sleepless nights and the busy routine of caring for a tiny baby, however great their regard was for the hospital and all the staff who had worked for the safe arrival of one more beautiful baby.

At lunch time, Sally wrapped herself in her cloak and wondered what had happened to the summer. Rain pelted down and made tiny rivers along the verges of the grass at the sides of the drive and Claud had his lodge windows tightly shut against the damp chill of the air. 'It must be twenty degrees colder,' said Charlotte. 'Did you get caught yesterday?'

'Yes,' said Sally. 'I got caught in a storm.' She helped herself to a tray and joined the small queue in the cafeteria, as she had no time to wait in the main dining room. 'We'll have to hurry to make the lecture,' she said. 'I wish we could go into block as we did in training. But I suppose these interim lectures are good as Sister gives us a run-down on special cases.'

'She's really very good. I doubt if any other place has such a dedicated tutor. I learn a lot from her. You do know what she'll tell us about today?'

'No, is there something special?'

'I think we are in for a lecture about induction of labour—and how not to do it—as Dorian tried last night, and failed.'

'Is Sandra all right?'

'She's fine. She's back in bed with her lump still intact and Mr Dillinger says she'll come into labour naturally in about three days.' Charlotte laughed. 'I don't think Dorian had bargained for Sandra. She took one look at the equipment and said, "You aren't putting that up me. You'll hurt the poor little bugger".'

'She said that? I thought she hoped that the baby would die . . . or just go away before she had to see it.'

'Surprise! Our Sandra suddenly went all protective and seems to be looking forward to seeing her offspring.' They moved up the line and took soup and rolls. 'Good to eat something hot. I'm freezing now I've stopped rushing around. Come on, we can chat later.'

Sally Ashford followed her to an already crowded table and found that there was no need for her to make any contribution to the conversation. Yes, she thought, I'm back as if I'd never been away, if it wasn't for certain matters that had turned her heart and her life upside down. The hot soup burned her lip . . . so different from the cold salad she had unpacked from the cool box yesterday on the bank of the canal. 'Mayonnaise or French dressing?' she'd asked as she sat on her feet with the food set out before her.

'You think of everything . . . it's just too sad that all this wasn't really intended for me,' Matthew Tregonna reclined on the grass, regarding her lazily with mocking eyes. 'I wonder how it went in that devious little brain?' He looked up at the sky and folded his hands under the back of his neck, looking like a Greek god by a holy spring, his hair alive with sunlight and his face in a half smile.

'I had nothing to do with it. My mother has an overdeveloped sense of hospitality and she insisted that I should pack this for whoever was kind enough to give me a lift.'

'Ouch!' he said.

'It was kind to offer a lift, but even you didn't know just who would be accepting your offer, so it could have been two quite different people here today.' He turned to face her. 'Well, that's true, isn't it?' she said. 'I think that next time, I'll put my name—it might be better knowing who is accepting your lift and then you can make some excuse to refuse me. Or I shall find out whose car is the number on the list.'

'I'll have French dressing,' he said. 'I enjoy my food and this looks absolutely delicious, and I've no intention of letting you ruin my appetite.' He smiled with such warmth that she had to put a hand on the ground beside her to steady herself. 'Peace while we eat, and ever more, if you can bear it?'

'Peace,' she said and tried to laugh naturally. The

food was good and, as she watched him, she wondered which was the real Matthew Tregonna . . . the arrogant man who swept along the hospital corridors as if he was someone with supernatural powers with no need to be polite to lowly pupil midwives like Sally Ashford, or was he sometimes as he seemed now, with his hair untidy and his firm mouth relaxed in a lazy smile? She listened as he told her about the village at the back of the canal. 'Why did you come this way?' she asked. 'I thought you had a visit to make.' The suspicion that he was not being honest with her remained through the haze of wonder that surrounded her, having him all to herself in such surroundings, smiling and being attentive—as if he really liked her.

'My godparents live in the farm on the other bank. I thought we could pack up the lunch and lock the car and walk along the bank to the next bridge which gives direct access to the farm.' She relaxed. He hadn't brought her to this lovely but lonely spot for any other reason than to see some elderly people who would welcome a visit. She dismissed the vision of her own nakedness in the university swimming pool and the sombre eyes that had matched her dive down after her bikini top which was slowly moving further away to the bottom of the pool. At the time there had been no moment for analysis of his expression, but during the night when she had been unable to rest, she had construed his reaction as one of veiled desire, or not quite veiled lust. She told herself that any man would have reacted in the same way, and men like

Dorian would have been a greater embarrassment, and now, he must have forgotten the picture of the girl with streaming wet hair and a face bedewed with tear-like drops and utter misery in her eyes.

He was eating strawberries with a plastic spoon, after sprinkling them heavily with castor sugar. Sally laughed. 'My mother said I was to use this, but as you're driving, I'll have it all.' She held out a small bottle of liqueur.

'Kirsch? The woman's a miracle. What a lucky man your father must be.' He took the bottle and dripped the liquid on to the strawberries. 'Very clever as we have no cream to go with them.'

'Don't speak with your mouth full,' said Sally. 'I shall definitely find out who is offering lifts in future. I'll choose someone who doesn't eat everything in sight!' It was becoming easy to be natural, to make silly jokes with greater confidence, to trust him. I have this moment, she thought, with the sun shining and a lark singing with joy in the wheat field. I have his smile to remember and the intoxicating touch of his hand.

He held the vacuum flask to pour coffee and she watched the sinews of his hand tighten. That hand had fastened the clasp on her bikini top with a gentleness mixed with such sensuality that she had fled from his touch. She saw him looking at her with eyes that were enigmatic, as if he had his own private thoughts. He handed her the cup and their eyes seemed unable to look away. She bent her head and hid her expression, because in that moment of truth she knew that she wanted him as she had never wanted anything in her life, and that if he wanted her there would be no hope of resisting him. A flood of rising desire made her breathe fast and she wondered how the birds could sit so calmly on the water and not be frightened away by the beating of her heart.

She closed her eyes against a sudden darkness. I hope I'm not going to cry, she thought, but the darkness was nothing to do with tears. Mechanically, she made her hands gather the picnic remains and Matthew carried the box to the car. He came back to the rug and put his arms round her, drawing her to his body with relentless gentleness. She gasped and tried to push him away, but his lips stifled any word she might say, any protest, and her body refused to protest as she sank back on to the rug, his arms tightly round her, his mouth on hers in a long kiss of such infinite sweetness and pain that she wondered how she would live through the experience.

The darkness deepened. This is what it is like to want someone . . . it's like falling into a dark pit, but surely the stars or the sun should be shining above . . . ? She blinked as he put her away slightly to gaze at her face. The sky was dark and getting darker. She shivered slightly and he ran a finger down the angle of her shoulder towards the curve of her breast. A huge drop of warm rain fell on her face and she put up a hand to brush it away, breaking the spell. Another and another drop fell and the face of the canal grew angry and turbulent, as heavy thundery rain drenched the thirsty bank and drove sharp lances into the water. Matthew Tregonna looked up as if waking from a dream, an almost comical expression of rage on his face. 'Hell!' he said, and dragged her to her feet. 'The gods are angry,' he shouted against the wind that had come like a fury along the valley. 'Quick, get to the car. He bundled the wet rug into a ball and followed Sally, but they had both forgotten that the car was locked, ready for them to walk to the other bridge.

'Hurry up,' said Sally as he fumbled in his pocket for the car keys. Water ran down her face and on to her soaking shirt, outlining the thin bra under it. Her legs were wreathed in wet drapes and the sandals that had been so cool and dry were like soaking cardboard. He unlocked the back doors and thrust her in. She looked surprised.

'I'll drive to the farm and you can change there. No, sit in the back . . . I have to concentrate on the driving.' She glimpsed his set face in the mirror and smiled slightly. He looked as if he had been in the canal, not just caught in a storm. Thunder echoed down the waterway and lightning split the clouds. The windscreen wipers moaned as they tried to deal with the sheet of water driving against the glass and the car oozed slowly back to the village.

Matthew took the car along a lane behind the church and into a farm yard. A wet dog barked at them as the car stopped and Matthew ran to the front door, leaving his passenger in the car, to shiver and wonder what might have happened if the god of thunder hadn't intervened. Ashamed at her own abandoned response to his kisses, she knew that he had brought her to that lonely spot only to seduce her. She sent up a silent prayer of thanks that she had emerged intact and, as if to make excuses for her own behaviour, she began to blame him as the cynical, self-willed man she had first thought him. He had no real feelings of love, he had never mentioned love. He had seen her in the pool and wanted her and thought she was fair game . . . possibly thinking that he wasn't the first to succeed with her after the horse play in the nurses' home with Dorian, and the jealousy and possessiveness of Brian when they spoke on the telephone.

He thinks I'm an easy lay, she thought, unhappily, and wished that she didn't feel so cold. He seemed to be taking his time. She unfastened her soft grip which was in the back of the estate car and rummaged inside for dry clothes. She found a towel and thankfully rubbed her hair and face and the bare neck where it showed above her shirt. The soft material clung and she recalled one of the doctors at her training school saying of a woman in out-patients, dressed up to impress him when he examined her, "Her blouse was so tight, I could see not only the nipples but every Montgomery Tubercle round them". That's how I feel, she thought, and glanced at the silent building to see if Matthew or the owner was in sight. She peeled off her shirt and thrust it on the seat beside her, on the towel. It was soaking. She found a fresh tee shirt and after a moment's hesitation and another quick look outside, she added her wet bra to the discarded shirt and struggled into the clean dry top.

Matthew Tregonna ran back to the car. 'They're out,' he said. 'God! I'm wet.' He opened the rear door and rummaged for his case. 'I'm going to change in the barn . . . coming?'

'No thanks, I can manage here,' she said in a low voice.

He brushed the wet hair from his eyes and grinned, seeing the soft lines of her pale blue cotton top. 'Women's Lib, I see. Sure you won't come into the barn?' The invitation was unmistakable and the meaning very clear.

'*NO*! For heaven's sake get changed and leave me alone. I want to get back to London.'

He stiffened. 'I'm sorry. I had the impression back there that you were quite willing to spend a pleasant hour . . . whiling away the time on a river bank.' He seemed insulted and, for a moment, Sally had a feeling that he had intended only the kiss and the passionate embrace, while she had shown clearly that she had thought he intended much, much more. He ran back to the barn and disappeared inside the dim depths of the old building.

Oh, how shall I face him when he comes back? Sally tore at her skirt and underwear, dried herself and dressed with some difficulty in the confined space, but was soon dry with fresh shoes on her feet and a warm cardigan over her cotton shirt. As she combed her hair, she tried to think clearly. He had done no more than any red-blooded man would have done in the same circumstances. If I had been with Brian, we would have kissed, she thought, and knew with growing shame that it was her own awareness, her own mounting desire that had made this encounter seem quite different from all the other casual outings with boy friends. It was my fault. He just took what came easily. He must have seen that I wanted him, and I shall never know if he would have . . . taken me . . . completely. The guilt made her sit straight in the passenger seat, having spread the wet clothes on her towel, leaving a space for any that Matthew might want to add to the collection in the hope that the worst of the wetness would be gone before they arrived in London. He must believe that I am experienced—to return his kisses with such passion—an experienced little tramp. Hadn't he hinted as much when she'd made that crack about the dog not knowing the difference between a friend and . . . a tramp?

A cold hand pushed past her shoulder as Matthew Tregonna flung his wet clothes into the back of the car on top of the neat array that Sally had left. He put his case in the back and slammed down the hatchback. Without a word, he got into his seat and started the engine. 'Let's get some heat going,' he said. 'If you're as cold as I am, you'll need it.'

'A pity that your friends were out,' began Sally.

'I knew that was coming,' he said, sourly. 'I just knew it! I suppose you think that I had no intention of seeing them? I suppose you think that I brought you all this way from the motorway just to have the pleasure of eating with you and enjoying any other pleasures you had to offer.' His voice was hard with a kind of sorrowful anger, and she couldn't decide if it was directed solely at her or if he was ashamed of his own behaviour.

'I have no idea what you had planned,' she said, coldly. 'I am not interested in your friends, if they exist or live at the farm, and I assure you I had nothing more than food to offer you . . . believe it or not.'

'Somewhere, I think we've got our lines crossed,' he said, stiffly. 'Let's drop the subject and concentrate on getting back to something worthwhile . . . work.'

'All right,' said Sally in a small voice. 'And I'm sorry if you thought I was rude.'

'You weren't. I think we were both thrown by sheer physical discomfort,' he said, but whether he meant the discomfort of getting thoroughly drenched or the discomfort of frustrated love, he gave no sign. 'I wonder if Lucy Trevor had her baby?'

Sally felt absurdly grateful for the change of subject. 'Oh yes, didn't you know, she had a lovely baby girl the night before I came home.'

'You weren't on duty were you?'

'No, but she was on my mind and I slipped up to the ward before I caught the coach to Bristol. She deserved to have a live baby.'

'So many women want children and can't have them, and yet there are still many women who can have them easily and try to avoid a family or have illegitimate babies. It's unforgiveable to bring a baby into the world without having a decent home for it.' He looked sternly ahead. 'The girl in the terrible nightdress—Sandra White—she can't wait to get it over and back to the bright lights. But at least she will provide a healthy infant for some lucky childless couple.'

They talked shop all the way back to Beatties, finding safety in the impersonal subject, and Sally was increasingly aware that she had expected more than he had intended and that his principles would never allow him to take a woman in a way that could endanger her in any way. The thought did nothing to console her, but only convinced her further that he must think she had been leading him on and now he despised her even more than he had done on the earlier occasions when she appeared at a disadvantage.

The run through the puddles with a bundle of wet clothes had cut through any polite goodbyes they might have exchanged. Sally heard herself call, 'Thanks for the lift,' and he answered briefly, closing the door behind her and starting up the engine to drive round to the car park.

'Come on, eat up.' Charlotte's voice broke into her thoughts. 'I have to go to the home first. Meet me by the lift and we can sit together.' She went away and Sally gathered her note books and text books together before going slowly to the outer corridor. She looked at the noticeboard by the entrance and read without enthusiasm that the table tennis tournament had been cancelled because the judge had 'flu. There was a concert for which tickets could be obtained free—that was better; a free pass available to a gallery in the West End and a list of changes of staff.

This was fresh and she studied it with mild interest until she came to the last item. "Owing to the mild epidemic of Streptococcal infection in the baby unit at Redlake Hospital, the unit has been cleared and the staff tested. The carrier has been found and two suspects isolated. Three pupil midwives will take their places until throat swabs are clear." 'Oh, *no*!' she said.

'What's that?' said Charlotte. 'Come on, we can check for free tickets later.'

'Stop and look for a minute. Do you see that?'

'I don't believe it. I was due to do night duty here.'

'I've heard it's like Colditz there and they all hate the Sister Tutor.'

'We'll get good experience, though. We shall get to the labour ward more quickly and be miles ahead of our set when they come. I'm glad we're both going,' said Charlotte. 'I like Violet, too. She will be fun to have around. You, Vi and me . . . so watch out, Redlake.'

They were panting slightly as they slipped into seats in the back row of the lecture theatre. Sister Beringer was not at her desk so they breathed easily again. Charts of the human body and a blow-up of a pregnant uterus complete with coiled up foetus were lit by strong white lights and neatly-covered trolleys were ready for demonstration. Sister arrived looking rather cross. 'Are you all present? I have no intention of repeating anything so you must listen and ask questions about anything you don't understand.'

In seconds, the class was quiet and attentive, recognising the genius of the woman who taught them so well. In spite of her private feelings for the woman, Sally knew that they'd be very lucky indeed if they ever found a better teacher. But this might be the last lecture she heard from Sister Beringer. This would be the last day at Beatties for a long time, until the powers that be decided to send her back to finish her stint in the wards there.

I shall never see him again. It came like a blow. Never to see that disturbing face, to feel those deep-set eyes regarding her with appraisal . . . approval or dislike. Never to feel the touch of his hand on hers, even in a working situation when to him it would be no more thrilling than the touch of a pair of forceps, never to hear his voice or feel the touch of his mouth on hers.

'Nurse Ashford?' Sally blinked and sat up straight.

'Yes, Sister.'

'I hope that you will listen more closely to Sister Blake at Redlake hospital.'

'I was listening, Sister.'

'Tell me what I was saying.'

'Describe the apparatus for Sandra,' hissed Charlotte.

'For interuterine catheterisation for the induction of labour, a trolley is needed with the induction drip apparatus and fluids containing . . .'

she went on to give details, remembering the things that Nurse Cary had told her and the containers of fluid she had been shown.

'Very good,' said Sister Beringer, dryly, 'Especially as I hadn't come to the actual fluids used, but had only described the apparatus. I see that one of you has extra sensory perception.' She smiled. 'I'm glad to see that you were keen enough to pick up the facts from the ward routine,' she paused. 'It's a pity that some of you will have your lectures disrupted here, but Matron says that she has no alternative but to send three of you to Redlake. I think you know who is going and the minibus will be ready at the gates at ten a.m. tomorrow. You will have to clear your rooms completely as the girls from Redlake will come here as soon as they are free of infection.'

'But I thought we were busy here, Sister. Surely Redlake isn't any busier than Beatties?' said Charlotte.

'At the moment, there are more medical students there doing their midwifery course, which means they have as many deliveries as possible so that they can get their individual quotas. The mothers go to a post-natal unit as soon as there is no risk to mother or baby, and the students follow up by daily visits to finish the cases, but the labour ward is very busy— too busy, judging by this outbreak of infection.'

She went on to say that they must get enough sleep and fresh air as the work would be hard and conditions not as good as at Beatties. 'I don't want to see you back here for the wrong reasons, like throat infections, but we shall miss you all.' Charlotte saw that Violet Bastable was smiling. 'Please leave all borrowed text books in the library before you leave. The library at Redlake is . . . adequate,' said Sister.

'Something tells me that she doesn't really like Redlake any more than the nurses do,' said Charlotte. 'Sounds as if it might be fun. Masses of gorgeous men about to while away our exhausted off-duty.'

'We shall be quite oblivious to anything but bosoms and bedpans and babies,' said Violet, with a gurgling laugh, 'but if we have time, I shall hire a bicycle to explore the Heath. I heard that it is in a very pretty place.'

'A wobbly bicycle after a day on the wards? Count me out, Violet my angel. Invite me only if you find a man with a Merc. to take us cloud riding.'

A dusty estate car would be enough, if the driver could ever look on me with anything but amused contempt, thought Sally.

CHAPTER EIGHT

'I SUPPOSE that this is what life is all about,' said Violet Bastable, smiling down at the tiny baby she held in her arms. 'He is a very handsome young man, isn't he?' The grateful young mother beamed with delight and put out her arms to take the baby for feeding. Violet sat on the edge of the bed to settle the baby in a comfortable position and then hurried back to the nursery for the next baby.

'Two more to give out and three weighings, then we collect them up again. It's all go, Vi.' Sally Ashford smiled at the happy-looking West Indian nurse who had gone with her and Charlotte Davenport to the Redlake Hospital in the country outside London.

'I'm really happy with the babies,' said Violet. 'I never want to do any other kind of nursing. I just love to see the mothers when they see the babies for the first time—it's like a little miracle every time we have a new baby in the nursery.'

'You'd better watch it, Vi. You'll end up married with at least ten children of your own.'

'I couldn't wish for a better fate . . . if the right man asks me.' She scooped up another bundle in her competent brown arms and her sense of true joy was infectious. 'I'll just take her in and see how the slow feeder is doing, then we can do the weighings.'

The ward was fairly quiet as all the beds were full, and until three mothers left with their babies for the convalescent home the next day, there was just the routine of feeding, changing and weighing to be done at three or four hourly intervals, depending on the size, condition and age of the babies. Sally glanced at the clock. One more morning here and then . . . she took a deep breath. From two o'clock, she would be on duty in the labour ward, cleaning, preparing and watching deliveries for two days and then she would take her first delivery, a case that she would follow up from admission to delivery and for two days after the first bathing of the baby and the first post-natal examination of the mother to see that everything was back in place, and that she had suffered no injury during birth.

'Ideally, you should see your patients again in post-natal clinic in six weeks time to make the final examination, checking for muscle weakness or pro-lapse of the uterus,' said Sister Blake. 'Un-fortunately, the patients come from all over the area and will attend the clinics where they had their ante-natal care and where they attended relaxation classes.'

'Do many mothers have to have treatment, Sister?' Charlotte had asked.

'No, with good labour-ward care and the right ante-natal examinations, it is easier to check for possible complications before they happen. We know, for example, that a woman with a baby in a certain position before birth will take longer to deliver than one in another position . . . but you have seen the demonstrations in the lecture room, I hope.'

'Yes, Sister Beringer showed us on the model.'

'If we know that labour might be long, we can make sure that the mother has plenty of rest and sleep even when she is in the first stages of labour. In that case, we have a woman who isn't exhausted when she arrives in the labour ward. This is important as the word labour speaks for itself. Having a baby is hard work . . . labour. If the mother is too tired, the muscles can't do their job and push when the time is right. As soon as second stage arrives, when we *want* the mother to push instead of holding back and panting, when the cervix isn't sufficiently stretched in first stage, it is essential that she can *really* push and not run the danger of uterine inertia.' She smiled. 'I didn't mean to give you a lecture in the ward, but we have to deal with questions as they crop up or we'd never get through all you need to know. Six months isn't long enough, in my opinion.'

'I think she's good,' said Charlotte, later. 'I was half afraid of Sister Beringer, but I don't mind asking questions here.'

'I hear she gets very bad tempered in the labour ward,' said Violet.

'If things go wrong, I think I'd be bad tempered,' said Charlotte. 'You have the lives of two people to consider, the mother and the baby. I think you're lucky, Sally, to be first to go into the labour ward.'

'You make it sound as if I'm in first stage, myself,'

said Sally, laughing. She heard her own laughter and was amazed how contented she was at work. This is the answer, she thought. I can work and get tired, when there will be no time for dreaming. She still imagined the face of the man who had taken her heart and torn it with doubts and guilt and self reproach . . . and anger. He was in every white coat she saw, in every masculine laugh in the corridors. I love this work and I know that this is what I was seeking. I shall never go back to general nursing after this. 'Are you going to book up for second part?' she asked.

'Good grief, let's get this lot over first,' said Charlotte.

'I'm going to,' said Violet. 'This is what I want to do. I would like to work in a maternity hospital in England for a year and then go home. They need good midwives and special ante-natal care in some of the villages.' Already, she was back in her sunny islands, in her dreams, with a worth-while skill to give to them. Lucky Vi, to have life so planned, so clear cut and so happy.

'Let's write to a few places together,' said Sally.

'And what if that nice Brian whisks you off to get married first,' said Charlotte.

'Brian?' Sally looked blankly at her friend. 'He doesn't come into it at all.' If she had ever had doubts about Brian, she now knew that even if Matthew Tregonna never saw her again, or if he vanished from the face of the earth, she couldn't marry him. 'I love this work and I shall do it for as long as I am nursing—if I pass my exams. If not, I shall still work with maternity cases, in some capacity.'

Charlotte grinned. 'Somehow you don't convince me that you are a Florence Nightingale. For one thing, you're much too sexy. Even your initials—you must have been teased about that—S.A. . . . sex appeal.'

'I thought I'd left corny jokes back home in junior school,' said Sally, scathingly. 'I am dedicated to my profession,' she said, with dignity.

'Liar,' said Charlotte, cheerfully, and tucked a red-faced baby into its cot, where it proceeded to yell.

'Wind,' said Sally and Violet together and Charlotte had to pick the baby up and burp her before putting her down again.

'I could get fed up with you, Henrietta,' she said.

'She can't be called that?'

'No, but when I'm cross with them I call them all the names I hate. That baby boy over there who wet me all down my clean apron yesterday just before the consultant's round, I call Cholmondeley Spiv, because he looks like a high-class barrow boy.'

Sally giggled. 'I can't think that Sister will let us laugh like this in the labour ward. I shall miss you two nuts.' She watched Charlotte and wondered how her relatives would react to seeing their aristocratic daughter working so hard and loving it. 'Have you hired that bike yet, Violet?' she said. The sun shone on the weeping willow by the entrance to casualty. As Charlotte had said when she saw it first, a weeping willow was no advertisement for a hospital, but today the leaves moved softly, casting dappled shadows on the well-cut grass and the smell of grass cuttings came pungent and clean through the half-open window of the office. Sally turned her back on the sight, knowing that she had to work until the sun had gone down and the colours had died.

The labour ward had been shown to the new student midwives as soon as they arrived. For once, it was empty except for the quickly moving nurses who cleaned with feverish intensity, knowing that at any moment the telephone might ring announcing yet another admission in labour. Two medical students were helping with the trolleys as part of their training, and they looked rather resentful. 'It's no use you looking at me like that,' said Sister. 'What happens when you are in General Practice and you are confronted with a delivery? Eh . . . what do you do without a team of highly-trained nurses? I'll tell you,' she said without waiting for a reply. 'You either cope very well with the little you have on hand, because you have learned to do it here, *or* . . . you make a mess of it, use unsterile or unwashed utensils and run a risk of infection.'

'Yes, Sister,' they said, and began to help a little more willingly.

And now, Pupil Midwife Sally Ashford found herself standing by the sink in that labour ward, washing the suction apparatus and making sure that there were no obstructions in the tubing before it was sterilised. One of the students was washing the table on the right of the theatre. Sally smiled. He had been the least willing on his first day but was now washing every crevice with antiseptic as if his life depended on it as well as the lives of his patients. Sally wondered what had happened to make him change his attitude and suspected that Sister's waspish tongue had a lot to do with it.

'Where's the small autoclave?' Sally asked him.

He jerked a hand over his shoulder. 'In the next room to the sluice,' he said, and stood up. 'God, I've slipped a disc,' he said.

'Rubbish,' said Sally. 'Do you good . . . I'm sure you'll get no sympathy from Sister if you say that to her.' She smiled. 'How many have you delivered?'

'Two so far and there's one lady puffing away nicely in the admission room. That's the reason for my hard work.' He looked at Sally. 'I had no idea that the nurses worked so hard. I shall have a far greater respect for you all in future. We're so used to going on ward rounds with our bosses and seeing everything immaculate that few of us spare a thought for the trouble you've taken.'

'We'll forgive you if you'll remember that when you are a consultant. I shall expect you to leave beds tidy after examination and to be tolerant if the ward is busy,' said Sally, half in fun.

'It shall be,' he said, solemnly. 'I'm Mike Attron, and I believe that if you are the legendary Sally Ashford, we are doubling up for work and off-duty.'

'Oh, are we?'

'Now, don't get worried, I'm brighter than I

look.' He glanced around to see if Sister was about. 'I heard a rumour that we are to go on the night shift with two midwives in here.'

'Already? But I haven't done one delivery yet.'

'Not a word. I'm not supposed to know, but be ready in a couple of days.' He smiled. 'At least I shan't have Sister barking at me round every corner.'

'You haven't seen the senior midwife on night duty,' mocked Sally. 'But seriously, is it true?'

'Quiet,' he said. 'Better get that tube into the steriliser. I got a rocket the other day for taking too long and we need a couple more to keep in reserve here.' Sally left the room, amazed at the change in his manner and the powers of observation he now seemed to have developed, but it was all around her; the sense of being poised ready for action, the eager expectancy of every member of the staff who knew that they had an important role to play that only men and women with their specialist training could carry out with safety. It was a humbling thought, that in her as yet half-skilled hands rested the welfare of women and helpless babies.

The day progressed slowly and the staff began to grumble, as always, as soon as the unit was slack. There had been two deliveries the previous night, but an outsider would have imagined that they had been idle for days. Idle? They had cleaned every bit of equipment, the tables and trolleys and sterilisers, the walls and ceilings had been washed and the floors lay glistening damply and smelling of fresh disinfectant. The tiny cots, strung up at an angle so that the delivered infant could be placed head down to allow any mucus or obstructing fluid to drain from the mouth and nose and not to settle inside the tiny lungs, were ready with clean soft sheets and folded blankets, a drip stand by each one and an array of bottles, clearly labelled and filled with every fluid that might be needed for intravenous use, subcutaneous injection or cleansing. Sterile packets containing cut down sets of instruments and intravenous needles and canulae were ready, phials of drugs were on view behind the locked doors of the drug cupboard ready for use and the diathermy machine and emergency lights were being tested for the second time that day.

In one way it was good that a new nurse should have time to see where everything was kept, but having done general training, Sally had the skill and experience to know the most likely situation for all the drugs and apparatus in common use, and she longed to be able to make her first delivery. She took notes of all the pre-natal women, knowing that one of them would become her patient now that she was to be on night duty in the labour ward, but she didn't mention that she had heard the news, wisely waiting until she was told officially. With the noted facts of their ante-natal care safely in her case book, she went off duty and down to supper. It had been an interesting day and she had hardly had time to feel anything but interest for the work in hand.

'Hi!' said Charlotte. 'I hear that you are for night duty.'

'Yes, Sister told me as I went off duty. Unless

they call me for an emergency in theatre, she found out I'd done a lot of theatre work, I am to stay off duty tomorrow and go on tomorrow night at ten. That gives me time to sleep, or so she said, but I was never very good at first days sleep on night duty.'

'Have a good night tonight and a lie-in and go right through,' said Charlotte, with a grin. 'If you were out to a party, you'd be as late and have as little sleep before duty, so I see no difference.'

'Talking of parties, have you seen the notice board?' said one of the other nurses. 'There's a disco on Saturday and a wine and cheese given by Matron in a week's time.'

'The old girl's birthday?' said Charlotte.

'No. The consultants are a cunning lot. They are short of good midwives both here and for their domiciliary staff, so they give a party to each new batch to let them know what a marvellous place this is.'

'And I suppose that when we have that precious certificate after our full year and we are ready for a job, we think, with tears of gratitude in our eyes, of the kind people of Redlake and apply for jobs here?'

'Something like that. You see, when you do your vivas, the consultant will let you know if you are any good by asking where you intend practising. They are all out to rake in the best ones.'

'But if I'm on night duty, I shall miss it.'

'No, the midwives cover for you with the help of staff from the wards.' The nurse looked envious. 'It's a better party than they give us and we have to change babies all evening!'

'You should do midder,' said Charlotte.

'Not my scene,' she said.

'Might be fun,' said Charlotte, glancing at the
suddenly sad face of her friend. 'Cheer up, you've
still got beautiful hair and long legs. I doubt if you'll
be left to languish by the record player.'

'It isn't that,' said Sally. 'Let's go out for a walk
before bed . . . could go as far as the local. One of
the students said it's quite good if you like stock-
broker-belt gothic.'

'There . . . you have a date already.'

'No, we were just talking.' They changed and
walked along the road, having to step on to the
grass verge when cars swept by, as the road was
badly edged with no pavements. The local hotel
glowed through the summer dusk and small bats
flew over the trees. A burnished moon rose to show
them the way and it was once more warm and
sultry. Sally looked up at the innocent sky and
remembered the last time she had trusted the
weather. A jacket lay folded over her arm, to the
amusement of Charlotte who set out in a light
blouse and jeans, but Sally recalled the deluge that
had interrupted her waterside interlude with
Matthew Tregonna just before she was sent down
to Redlake.

'I saw one of our men from Beatties,' said Charlotte. Sally felt her heart beat faster. 'Quite a
surprise. I thought we were in another world with
no contact with our past and who should walk in to
Sister's office but . . . guess who?'

'Who?' said Sally with dry lips.

'Mr Dillinger. I had forgotten that he liked to follow up any interesting cases that got transferred here. Nice man . . . he remembered my name and asked after you.'

'Did he?' Sally tried to hide her feelings. For one terrible moment, she had thought there could be only one man from Beatties and that would be Matthew Tregonna. She told herself that there was no reason for him to come down to the country when he was so busily engaged in his work in London. But Mr Dillinger was busy, too. There might be a time when he would send his next in line to check a patient if he was too busy to come, personally. 'Did he say anything about anyone at Beatties, any patient we know, I mean,' she added, hastily.

'No, except that Sandra had a baby girl and refuses to let her go for adoption. Anyone would think that she had planned for the baby and wanted it badly. It's strange how they change once the baby is born, and mother-love refuses to be denied.' They settled at a small table in the corner of the vast over-decorated lounge.

'I'll get some cider,' said Sally. 'Hungry?'

'Of course. Let's have a pizza.'

They began to eat and looked round at the other customers. There were several people from the hospital who they knew by sight, two parties of men who hurried through their snacks before going into the other bar to play darts, some families and four or five very well dressed business men who propped up the bar and talked in overloud voices, eyeing the bar-person's low neckline and ogling every good-looking female in the room. 'Oh, sugar!' said Charlotte. 'Our local is full of twits like that. Do you wonder I keep away?'

'I thought you were going to exchange one lot of twits for another . . . what happened about Dorian? Did you have such a row that he won't take you home when you go?'

'My weekend has to wait. I volunteered and Sister thought I was one of the blessed martyrs. I felt quite guilty. Little does she know that I hate going home and was glad of an excuse to stay. It means I shall have some leave that I can add up to use for a trip to somewhere better. I thought I might fly off to Jersey to friends I had at school. And to answer your question—Dorian is a pain in the neck and I'd rather not be involved.' She fiddled with her last morsel of pizza. 'Have you really finished with Brian? I like his photograph. When is he coming to see you?'

'You don't fancy *him*?'

'Why not? He sounds just what I need, someone steady and kind and very good looking.'

'I suppose he is . . . all that.' Sally sounded guilty. 'He's always been there and I suppose I've taken him for granted. He is a very nice person, Charlie, and thinking about it, I do know that you and he would get on well.' Her face cleared. 'Save some of the leave and come home with me for a few days when we finish the course or before we go back to Beatties to do the time left there.'

'Great . . . that gives me an appetite. That was better than it looked. I'm going to get a pie.'

Sally refused more food and when Charlotte came back she had not touched her second glass of cider. Charlotte slapped the plate on the table. 'I've probably made a great mistake. This is made of cardboard, I think, but here goes.' She chatted and noticed that Sally wasn't really listening. Was she regretting losing Brian? Was she having second thoughts now that another woman showed interest in him? She took a large bite of pie. 'I wonder if our Romeo will come to the party?' she said, indistinctly through the thick pastry.

'Romeo?'

'Our golden boy of the moods . . . Our Matthew.'

'He's the last person who'd come to a party like that,' said Sally. 'He's too full of himself to want the company of students.' Her cheeks were flushed and her eyes overbright and Charlotte gave her a long, cool, wondering look. 'Ready?' said Sally. 'I need some air.' They wandered on to the Heath and saw the waterlilies silver beneath the moon.

'What a waste,' said Charlotte. 'This is much too romantic for the likes of me . . . let's get back and play scrabble, take a cold bath or write a letter to an unfavourite uncle.'

Just because she could stay in bed late in the morning, it was irritating to be wide awake at the usual time for getting up and Sally tossed and turned in bed wondering what to do. If only she had a com-

panion to share the day it would have been bear-
able, but every time she closed her eyes and tried to
forget that there was nobody available from her
own set to spend the day with her, sleep eluded her
and the only fantasy she could summon up was one
face, tormenting her with its beloved, hated charm
and his irresistible strength. She imagined him as he
was that day on the canal bank, she saw him again
as he was on the ward and she imagined him with a
woman in his arms, a shadowy woman who bore no
resemblance to the girl he thought was a plaything,
a girl who would go with anyone who seemed to
admire her, or worse still, was engaged to one man
and two-timing him with others, reducing her to
nothing in the opinion of the high and mighty
Matthew Tregonna.

It was too much. She got up and dressed and went
out into the bright sunlight of a clear warm morning. She wandered away down the road and
watched the dragonflies darting between the osiers.
The day passed in a dream of unreality and she
hardly recalled eating before she reported on duty
at ten.

Michael was there already, gowned and masked.
'Hurry up,' he said. 'One of mine is ready and Night
Sister had a patient prepared who will probably be
delivered tonight. That's yours, Duckie.'

Sally hastily put on a gown and mask and went
into the labour ward to report. She was told to sit
with the patient in second stage and to administer
gas and air if required. Sally blessed the fact that
Sister Beringer had so expertly taught them all the

use of the apparatus. She smoothed the damp brow with a cool sponge and murmured comforting words. The woman relaxed, confident in her attendants, and clasping the hand of the girl whose name she didn't know, but who was to be her nearest and dearest friend for the next hour.

Mike looked calm but hot and he stood with his gloved hands in front of him as if they didn't belong on the ends of his arms but were some strange appendages that he had never seen before tonight.

The monotonous whine of the air-conditioning filter droned in the background and from the sterilising room the clunk of instruments indicated that another delivery trolley was being laid up. One of the midwives supervised the delivery and Mike proudly laid a scarlet and shrieking baby across the abdomen of the tired woman. She wept as she looked at the tiny hands that seemed to be striving towards her. Sally glanced at Mike's face and was glad for his sake that the mask hid most of it, as tears of relief and that strange birth exultation coursed down into the linen.

'What is your name, Doctor?' said the mother.

'Attron . . . Mike Attron.'

'Michael . . . that's nice. You don't mind, do you? I'd like to call him Michael.'

The midwife smiled as he took the baby to check the cord and to put him in the cot. 'He's on cloud nine,' she whispered. 'Don't tell him that eighty percent of the mothers here want to call their babies after a member of staff. They may change their minds later, but it's a nice thought.' She glanced towards the door. 'Scrub up, Nurse. And good luck. This is your case.' Sally almost ran to the scrubbing bay. She could hear the deep, stertorous breathing of a woman trying not to bear down as the contractions came faster and with greater intensity. One glance told Sally that the patient was Mrs Broker, a mother of two children who was hoping for a girl after having two lively boys. She remembered the notes and the times of labour noted for the other deliveries, and that with neither of the boys had she been in labour for long.

'Hurry up, Nurse,' called the midwife as Sally pushed the glove packet away and eased her fingers in the tight rubber. The patient was bearing down fast and already the tiny lock of hair showed as each contraction pushed the baby nearer the vulva. Black hair, thought Sally, forgetting that all hair looks dark when wet.

There was no time to feel inadequate, no time to be frightened. Concentrating on all she had been taught, it was almost as if Sister Beringer was behind her, telling her what to do. The baby's head was eased out and the tightly shut eyes cleansed quickly with the swabs put ready, the body followed with a swift movement and within ten minutes of scrubbing up, Sally held aloft a small but perfectly formed girl child who greeted the world with bubbles instead of cries. The staff midwife held the baby upside down and used the sucker to clear the mouth and nose, but taking care not to put the sucker end too far inside the delicate mucous membrane in case she injured it. Sally glanced anxiously

at the baby while she waited for the next contraction of the mother's now soggy uterus and, as it
came, making the womb grow tight and small, the
placenta slipped out, complete. The baby still
looked rather blue, even when the umbilical cord
was tied in two places and severed. Sally cleaned up
her patient while the midwife worked on the baby.
Suddenly, just when Sally thought it would never
happen and a wave of anxiety seemed to spread
through the labour ward, the child took a shuddering breath and cried, fretfully at first and then in
anger at being taken from the warm, moist womb
that had protected her for nine months.

The mother asked for the baby and it was given to
her. She didn't seem to notice the coating of creamy
vernix caseosa that covered her daughter, but saw
through what was in fact nature's mackintosh, pro-
tecting the foetus from the wet surroundings of the
womb, to the child for which she had longed . . . a
little girl. 'She's beautiful, she's beautiful,' she said,
over and over again.

Within minutes, all loss of blood from the mother
had stopped and she was wheeled back to the ward
to sleep and be ready to feed her baby in the morning. 'Get on with the washing,' said the midwife.
'The bathroom is free and Michael is doing his
baby.' Sally smiled. She had forgotten that every
student had to do the first bathing and dress the
stump of the umbilical cord so that it remained free
of infection and dropped away naturally on the fifth
to eighth day leaving a dry scar. The thought of
Michael bathing a tiny baby was absurd and when

she went into the bathroom, carrying the cot in which her own newcomer lay, she saw that he was still examining his baby for possible abnormalities.

'Surely you've had time to examine him by now?'

'I'm scared. Thank God you've come. Can we do them at the same time and I can see what you do?'

'Now do you believe Sister Beringer and Sister Blake?' teased Sally Ashford. 'What would you have done if this was a remote farmhouse?'

'I'm getting a good smart practice in the Smoke,' he said with feeling. 'No maternity cases.'

'Go on, you loved every minute. I watched you.'

'It was rather fun,' he said, sheepishly, 'But I never bargained for bathing the little tiddlers. They're so *small*! I shall drop him.'

Sally finished examining her baby for cleft palate, spina-bifida or any of the obvious deformities that could be found, if they existed, in this first examination, and prepared her bath. Michael watched and did the same, dragging his chair and table next to her and copying every movement she made until she began to hum a rather jazzed up version of "Me and my shadow" and he tried to get on alone. Neither of the babies cried in disgust and when they were clean and sweet smelling, with tiny dressings over the cord stumps. Sally took pity on Michael and said that if he'd write her notes, she'd dress both the babies, 'Just this once—you're on your own after this one.' A sudden suspicion crossed her mind. 'You've never done a bath, have you? Who did you bribe to do the others?'

'That would be telling,' he said, with a wink. 'I

have ways and means of getting my own way with willing nurses.'

'I shall tell on you if you don't behave. Seriously, Michael, you just have to do your own babies or you'll never learn.'

He was suddenly serious. 'That's why I'm very grateful to you. I learned more watching you do it well than I could from a dozen lectures. I shall do the rest, cross my heart, I swear it. I might even get to like it.' He picked up the sleeping baby. 'Marvellous, isn't it? I can't wait to show the mother. We are supposed to take them in for five minutes, aren't we?'

'Make sure the name tag is firmly on before you leave the labour unit . . . that's a must. I don't think we could get these two muddled—I think they might be a little suspicious if the one with the boy got the girl and vice versa—but mistakes have been known to happen in less well organised places and we can't afford to take chances.'

Proudly, they took their tiny bundles to the respective mothers, who sleepily stroked the tiny cheeks and then thankfully slipped into deep sleep, secure in the knowledge that the babies were born, in safe hands and would be there waiting for them as soon as they woke in the morning.

Sally cleared her trolleys and swabbed the labour ward floor while Michael cleaned instruments and checked sterile drums. I wonder if Matthew Tregonna ever had any difficulty bathing his first baby, she thought, and giggled. 'What's funny?' said Michael.

'Oh, nothing,' said Sally. 'One day when you are famous, a pupil midwife may wonder if you ever had difficulty bathing your first baby. It's hard to imagine men like . . . Mr Dillinger doing it, isn't it?'

CHAPTER NINE

SALLY ASHFORD sank on to her bed and sighed. 'If anyone had told me that I would deliver two babies on my first night on night duty and admit two more patients, shave and prepare them and do a round of bedpans and swabbings, as well as all the usual routine, I would have laughed.'

'They don't care, do they?' said Violet with a grin. 'Babies come just when they want to, not when we find it convenient.' She looked thoughtful. 'Except when people like Dorian get funny ideas and try to bend things. I heard Mr Dillinger telling Sister Blake about it. Sandra is coming down to the annexe to learn how to look after her baby before she goes home, and I suppose that Mr Dillinger didn't remember that I knew all about it when he talked so freely to Sister. He's very mad at Dorian and hopes to get him transferred to a research team as soon as he has done his quota of natural births. He'll do less harm among the test tubes than with patients.'

'I must make a point of seeing Sandra. Even if she is a bit off hand, I think she's had a hard life and it takes courage to keep a baby if you have very little to offer it in the way of a home and good food and clothes.'

143

'You look bushed. Let me make you a cuppa. I'm off this morning and we could go on the Heath for a bit before you go to bed.'

'Thanks, Vi . . . I'd like that,' yawned Sally, and went to have a shower after the long hot night. I was very lucky to have such easy deliveries for my first ones, she thought, and recalled the shocked expression on Michael's face when he knew that his next one would be a breech delivery. She'd left him scrubbed and gowned with no hope of being off duty for hours. 'Poor lamb, he'll be fit to drop,' she said.

'Ready, if you are,' called Violet Bastable, and when Sally went along to her bedroom she had mugs of tea and currant buns waiting. 'I know I shouldn't,' she said, helping herself to the biggest bun, 'but I get starving here. I could drink a bottle of milk if I got the chance when I'm mixing feeds, and then I'd be as big as a bus.' She sat complacently listening to Sally's account of the night, giggling when she heard about Michael bathing his first baby.

'Well, if I'm not to fall asleep here, let's go,' said Sally. She slung a pale blue linen jacket over her shoulders and brushed the crumbs from the crisp beige dress. Her eyes seemed deep-sunk with tiredness, and had the false brightness of the night worker. She was relieved to be going out with Violet, who was sure to make her laugh and take a rational view of life. Somehow, the sunshine of Violet's country and people had a warming effect on everyone with whom she came in contact, and she was very popular with nurses, doctors and patients.

'You need some air, and a dose of sun.' She laughed. 'You've got a bit of catching up to do to get my tan!'

They went across the Heath to the bigger of the two dew ponds that had matured into pretty lakes and were sometimes inviting enough to tempt the staff to risk an encounter with a leech or two and paddle round the pebbly edges. Bees worked among the flowers and Sally picked a bunch of harebells before sitting on the bank and watching the birds come down to drink the clear water. Violet went to pick young fern fronds which she insisted were good to eat and tasted like asparagus when cooked.

'That's not fern, that's bracken,' said Sally.

'Same thing, but I do know what is edible,' said Violet.

'Well, don't bother to get any for me. I'm going to soak up enough sun to make me eligible to play in your brother's steel band.' Sally settled on a soft bank and closed her eyes. She heard the bees and a lone blackbird trilling somewhere to her right, and then the waves of sleep folded over her like soft layers of silk, under which lay rows and rows of tiny babies all waiting to be bathed. She was running from one to another, trying to decide which to take, and a man in a white coat was shouting to her that she must do every one before she went to the wine and cheese party; a man whose face she couldn't see but whose voice was that of the man she might never see again, the voice of Matthew Tregonna. In her dream, she began to cry and slow tears dropped on the babies. She heard a murmuring and felt a firm hand on hers where it lay across her breast, clutching the harebells. A kiss, light as thistledown and as thrilling as the touch of pure silk against the skin, touched her cheek, her eyelids and, briefly, her lips. She stirred, unwilling to wake up now that the dream was good. She had a sensation of peace and of being enfolded with love, as if a beloved person had really kissed her . . .

'Wakey, wakey!' called Violet. 'I never saw such a person for dropping off. If you want something to eat before you go to bed, we'd better get back. I have to go on duty at two, so I could eat with you in the dining room.'

'What?' Sally was drunk with sleep and needed time to recover. 'I really did sleep . . . and I had such strange dreams.' She moved her hand and found that the harebells were gone. 'I was going to press them,' she said, stupidly.

'Press them?' Violet laughed. 'Shall I take you to a dream merchant to unravel that lot?'

'That wasn't a dream, I had some harebells that I tied up with cotton and wanted to press for my mother. She collects dried flowers and there aren't any really big harebells on the Downs at home.' She looked about her, rather crossly.

'Don't worry about it . . . just look around, girl. Thousands of them everywhere.' Violet picked half a dozen and handed them to Sally. 'I'll pick more if you want.'

'Let's eat in the snack bar across the way. I feel too fragile to go into the dining room.'

Violet made a face. 'It's very convenient having the pub right by the Heath, but I'd rather go back today. It's one thing having our lot talking shop, but it would be worse in there.'

'Why?'

'You didn't see him?' Violet shook with laughter. 'Perhaps he missed you among the heather.'

'Who? Come off it, Vi, you're having me on.'

'That beautiful man from Beatties is having lunch with someone from Redlake and Mr Dillinger.'

'What beautiful man?'

'Don't look so stricken. It doesn't concern you as you say he leaves you cold. That nice hunk of Tregonna. He saw me by the water and came over. I said you were taking a nap in the sun and he told me he was having lunch with the VIPs and went back. I thought he would have fallen over you on the way.'

'The dining room, definitely the dining room!' said Sally. The dream . . . how much had been dream, how much her own desires and . . . how much could have been reality? She put a finger on her cheek, there where the soft kiss had fallen. She touched her lips and wondered if the dream man had found them soft and warm, and she put Violet's harebells inside her handbag and wondered where the others were.

The day was cloudy with dreams and it was a relief to get dressed and go on duty that night. The ward was busy again and as soon as she had checked the charts of her deliveries she peeped in at the babies who looked disappointingly like all the others in the nursery, instead of having an aura of "Sally Ashford delivered me" round each tiny head. Michael wasn't to be seen. He had been given permission to stay off duty until midnight as he had remained on the ward long after the night staff had gone that morning. His breech took a long time to be born, as at least half an hour has to elapse between the body being delivered and the head, letting the head come very slowly, so that the soft bones of the skull wouldn't be torn during birth. It had been a very long second stage and Michael had waited to get his case safely in his notes.

'Lucky thing,' Sally said to the staff midwife. 'I wonder if I shall have a breech? Last night, I think the babies delivered themselves. Apart from seeing that everything was there and cutting the cord, I was quite unnecessary.'

'Don't wish anything more exciting on yourself. The next one might well be a Caesarian. She's been in labour for twelve hours and isn't far on yet. There was some talk in ante-natal of her having a slightly flattened pelvis and the baby is having trouble finding the best way down. If she doesn't get on any further, we shall ask someone to take the baby.'

'What about forceps, Nurse?'

'No, the head's too high, and we can't give much relaxant at this stage in case the womb contracts in the wrong places and makes it even more difficult.'

Sally found that as soon as she was working, her tiredness left her, and she was bright and energetic.

'Keep an eye on her, Nurse Ashford. I must ring Mr Dillinger to see if he will look at her before he goes back to town. Lucky he had to come down today. The theatre staff like him better than the man on call for Redlake, and he enjoys working here occasionally.' Sally sat by the patient, helping her to relax as each rather weak contraction came. It was evident that she was not making good progress and might need help. Not for the first time, Sally was glad to be training where every care was taken in the ante-natal stages of a pregnancy, so the hospital unit could know each patient and the patient would be familiar with the staff in the event of anything but a normal birth routine presenting itself. She did a routine check of blood pressure, pulse and respiration and listened to the steadily beating foetal heart, bringing a powerful stethoscope to the patient so that she could listen to her own baby's heart beat and know that everything was all right.

The woman dozed and stirred as each contraction began, but there was no progress and when the staff midwife came back, Sally shook her head. 'Go down to supper, Nurse, and then lay up for a Caesar in the theatre. You know what is needed, don't you?'

'Yes, Nurse. I was in a gynae theatre for three months and scrubbed for three Caesars and laid up for several more. Do you know who will be doing it?'

'I rang Mr Dillinger and he said he'd come in to see her. He also said that he used the same equip-

ment and drugs as they use here so that doesn't
make life difficult.' She closed the ward door,
softly. 'Just as well I rang him. He was leaving for
London in half an hour, having seen the people he
came to interview and the new patients with odd
symptoms that the consultant here thought might
interest him. If he hadn't been available, we would
have had to endure the new registrar.'

'What's wrong with him?'

'Not in the first class, but nice. However, I'd
rather have a bad-tempered surgeon who knew
what he was doing than a pleasant man who
operated with limp fingers.'

'Mr Dillinger isn't bad tempered in the theatre, is
he?'

'Let's say he doesn't suffer fools gladly, and nor
does his registrar. I've seen our Matthew fling
swabs from one end of the theatre to the other when
a nurse bungled the final check and they had to
keep the patient anaesthetised for longer than
should have been necessary, while they looked for
one swab.'

'I suppose he was justified,' said Sally, re-
luctantly, 'but why is it that everyone says "our
Matthew" in that way as if they let him get away
with anything because they like him?'

'Well, it's true. He's very well liked and the
patients adore him.'

'They see only one side of him when he's on his
best behaviour, but I think he's very rude, very
demanding and a bit of a menace.'

'Don't tell me that he has made a pass at you? I

thought it was only people like Dorian Warner who did that on duty.' She looked at Sally quizzically. 'I heard a rumour that you were seen out in a car with him . . . did he try it on?'

'No,' said Sally, quickly. 'I put my name down for a lift from Bristol and it turned out to be him. He brought me home, that's all.'

'My friend rang me from Beatties and she said he was somewhere in the country, far from the motor-way.'

'He had to see his godmother so he made a detour,' she said, shortly.

'Lucky old you to have him to yourself for so long. There are nurses who would give a year of their training for one date with him, but he doesn't seem to notice them.'

'He must have a girl friend somewhere,' said Sally.

'He did once, but I think she two-timed him when he was busy doing his first house surgeon's stint. Some women can't come to terms with the life and he didn't seem all that upset at the time. I suppose men with his charisma can afford to wait for Super-woman.' She sighed. 'He can ask any girl he fancies to go to the hospital dances and he does, never taking the same girl twice running. Maddening, isn't it?'

'At least you know where you stand,' said Sally. She made an effort to laugh. 'Well, that lets me out of the running. I've had my one rationed outing with sir. He will make quite sure we don't even speak to each other at the party if he comes . . . do you think he will?' She couldn't resist asking, even though she knew that if he ran true to form he would take a fresh partner, and they would wander over the Heath after the party and he would make love to her, knowing that women were like putty in his hands. She blushed as she recalled her ready response to his kisses. It must happen all the time and how he must laugh at the girls who let him pick them up for one evening and then drop them like hot coals as soon as he had proved to himself that he still had his full powers of seduction.

As she laid up the instruments she wondered how far he would have gone with her if the thunder storm hadn't cooled his ardour. And I would have let him take me, she thought, with shame. I wanted him, and I still want him, but now I know that I have control of myself and will never let myself be put in that position again. She covered the trolley with a sterile towel and went into the operating theatre to make sure that the nurse on duty had put out everything likely to be used. She checked the covered dishes of sterile syringes, ready for use at a moment's notice. One dish in a corner, labelled Ergometrine, for use as soon as the baby was taken from the uterus, to make the muscles contract quickly, so reducing the size of the empty womb and making sure that all bleeding from the site of the placenta stopped at once. Another contained a heart stimulant and yet another an ampoule of blood coagulant in case of haemorrhage. These were kept at specific points in the theatre with one nurse in charge of each in an emergency, knowing exactly the place where one drug could be found and not being able to give the wrong drug at the wrong time.

Everything was well done and she went back to the labour ward to see what needed doing there. Michael had arrived and was taking notes from a woman who had arrived in labour at the hospital outpatients having not attended any ante-natal clinics and having done no relaxation exercises. 'Glad you're here. I'm hopeless at telling them they're all right. I think they see that I'm wet behind the ears and believe that I am going to louse it up.'

'Not quite the language for a budding obstetrician, is it, Michael, and you'd better not let Sister hear you referring to patients as "them".' She smiled. 'I'll get the trolley and prepare her. I'll even show you how you manage without leaving your patient in a pool of antiseptic after the preparation.'

'Cow,' he murmured, but smiled and looked less harrassed. It was a standing joke that when he washed a patient or a baby, they had to swim for safety from his watery efforts!

Sally stood by the side of the bed and washed the girl's face and hands, combed her hair and waited for the next contraction, telling her softly that she must pant through her open mouth as soon as it started and not to fight it. 'Go with it and it will just be a twinge, but if you fight it, you tighten up and it hurts.' She wondered if it was too late to help her, knowing that it took time and self discipline to learn how to enjoy labour and the delivery instead of clinging to the nearest hand and screaming.

'There isn't time for a bath, is there?' said Michael. 'I'll get the trolley if you'll clean her up for me.' He grinned. 'Go on, be a sport and I'll take you to the wine and cheese.'

'Big deal . . . I don't like cheese all that much.'

'They have other goodies and I'll even put on a tie in your honour.'

'That I must see,' she said. They worked together until the staff midwife beckoned to Sally. 'Is the theatre to be used, Nurse? It's all laid up ready.'

'So I see. I'll take over here with this one. If she gets restless, he'll need help, but you had better be in charge of the theatre. I can give you two nurses and Night Sister will come to see to the baby if the anaesthetist is busy.'

'Who is coming, Nurse?'

'I don't know. Mr Dillinger was vague. He said that he hoped to do it, but if he couldn't, I could leave the arrangements to him. Put out all sizes of boots, if that's what's worrying you.'

'That's the least of my worries,' she said, but the midwife had gone, leaving her with a strange theatre and not knowing who was coming to take the main part in the operation.

The house telephone rang and Sally could hear Night Sister answering it. She bustled along the corridor and poked her head inside the surgeons' room where Sally was checking that brushes and combs and white theatre boots were ready and that the tea tray was laid with cups and plates and a tin of biscuits for use after the operation. 'Ready, Nurse?' Sister glanced at the clock. 'The anaesthetist is coming now, so get the patient in there, and the surgeon will be here in fifteen minutes. I should get scrubbed and let the nurses help with the patient.'

Sister wrote "Mrs Taylor" in large letters on the list board and the time. "For Caesarian", she added. Sally called to the dirty nurse to stand by, ready to help her into her gown as soon as she had left the scrubbing bay. As she pressed the remote-control pedal that turned off the taps, she turned and took the sterile towel held out to her on the end of special forceps. She dried her hands and picked up a size 6½ pair of gloves from its marked packet and after powdering her hands with the special talc-free powder, she drew on the gloves with a satisfying click which showed that they were new and resilient and wouldn't tear easily as some gloves did after repeated sterilising reduced their efficiency. Well, this is it, she thought, her pulse quickening as it did at the beginning of every operation at which she had helped. Next to midwifery, surely this was the most thrilling aspect of her work.

She folded the top towel and handed it to the nurse for re-packing as it wasn't soiled but would need sterilising again before use. The instruments lay in regular rows and she broke an ampoule of catgut that would be used at some stage, even if the surgeon had his own ideas about closures and peritoneal sutures. Thick catgut would be needed to close the dense muscle of the womb and she checked the large muslin swabs that would be used to pack the cavity, with no danger of being lost inside, as on each tape was clamped a pair of artery forceps to hang outside the incision. Steps from the corridor leading to the surgeons' room told her that she must be quite ready. The anaesthetist helped the nurse to wheel the unconscious patient into the theatre, her head covered in a neat turban of towelling, and a tube running from the anaesthetic machine down to her trachea, ensuring a constant flow of whatever gases the doctor decided was right to ensure complete relaxation of the abdominal muscles.

Night Sister listened to the foetal heartbeat before the sterile towels were put in position over the bare abdomen. She nodded and the anaesthetist grunted. The taps stopped running in the scrubbing bay and Sally stood ready with a long-handled swab holder and swab soaked in mercurochrome, a red staining antiseptic used extensively at Beatties and Redlake for purifying the skin before the first incision was made. A hand took the swab without a word and painted the exposed area. Sally handed more sterile towels to make a border of purity through which the surgeon could work and as he handed her the swab holder, her fingers touched the gloved hand.

'Scalpel, Nurse,' said the well-remembered voice. She handed him one with a fresh keen blade and watched the hands that she loved grow tense. 'Everything ready? Who takes the babe? Drugs ready? Resuscitation trolley and cot? Swab count done?'

His voice was crisp and business-like, needing

fast answers and making the staff share in his own confidence. He raised an eyebrow and the anaesthetist gave a thumbs-up sign. Sally didn't see the first thin line of blood that followed the knife. She turned to her instruments to have the forceps ready to slap into the outstretched hand as she had learned to do without having to be told. She swabbed, handed, sucked out blood, and the uterus was there like a small balloon, exposed and throbbing with the life waiting to be released.

In another five minutes, the baby was out, the first deep stitches already going in and the baby ignored by the operating team while they concentrated on the mother. Swiftly, the wound was sewn, layer on neat layer, and the right drugs given. The anaesthetist took out his tube and put in a thin stomach tube, passing it down the nose so that it wouldn't interfere with swallowing but be available to suck out the gastric juices and wind and so save the strain on stitches if the patient was sick.

Matthew Tregonna straightened and smiled. 'Good,' he said as the baby cried and the mother began to show signs of regaining consciousness. 'Well done, everyone. We got that one out quickly. What is it?'

'A boy . . . what she wanted,' said Sister, 'So it was just as well you took it.' She laughed, with the almost hysterical relief that follows such operations. 'We all know that baby boys haven't the life force of the female!' It was her stock joke, but everyone laughed.

'You think so, do you, Sister?' His eyes smiled

over the mask and he looked at the back of the girl who had assisted him so well, but who was now busily stacking soiled instruments into the bowl of water at the back of her trolley. 'What do you think, Nurse . . . thank you for helping.' He doesn't know who I am, she thought. Perhaps he won't recognise me at all, with a mask up to my eyes and this ridiculous cap that threatens to fall over my eyes.

'Of course, I agree with Sister,' she said. He looked at her as if for the first time and she knew that he recognised her voice. 'I'll get these washed, Sister, and then if you'll excuse me, I'll get back to the labour ward. Staff Nurse said she wanted me back as soon as possible.'

She pushed the trolley past the surgeon who had taken off his mask and was regarding her with an enigmatic smile.

'Nurse Ashford—and to think I didn't know. There seems no end to your capabilities. Who would have thought we would meet here?'

She gave him a half smile that he didn't see as it didn't reach her eyes, and went on to the sink. Of course he must have known she might be there on duty. He knew she was at Redlake . . . she recalled Violet's words. Even if he'd forgotten that she was at the hospital, the meeting on the Heath would have jogged his memory, even though they didn't actually meet. He went into the surgeon's room where tea was ready. Sally refused Sister's invitation to join them, saying again that she was needed in the labour ward, but when the instruments were safely packed for sterilising, the drums checked and the drugs locked away, she drank the tea that Sister brought to her.

'They're going now. Just peep in to make sure they've left nothing of value. Mr Dillinger is terrible. He regularly leaves watches or pens here and forgets that he has done so.'

Sally peeled off her damp gown and saw that the theatre was being cleaned properly. She went into the surgeons' room and made a heap of the discarded gowns. On a chair was a folder of notes. She flicked open the cover to see who had left it, the surgeon, the house surgeon who had assisted on the other side, or the anaesthetist.

A name written in bold handwriting at the top of the first page told her to whom it belonged, but she didn't read the written words under the name. Her eyes couldn't look away from a piece of folded paper from which something protruded at one edge, something pressed between the paper, blue and fine, like sky blue silk, delicate as her dream on the Heath . . . She opened the paper, slightly. A tiny bunch of harebells, tied with a strand of cotton lay there, the colour as bright as when she had picked them.

CHAPTER TEN

'CAESAR babies have such pretty, rounded heads,' said Charlotte. 'The first baby I delivered had such a huge caput on his head where he had been pushing against his poor mother for hours that he looked as if he had been in a fight and his head seemed very long. It's gone down now and he's quite a poppet, but this one is my pet. I wish I'd scrubbed for the Caesar.' She put the baby on the mother's lap and smiled. 'How's the tum?'

Mrs Taylor smiled. 'I feel fine.' She winced slightly as she pulled herself up in bed a little higher. 'I almost welcome the odd twinge, Nurse. It tells me how lucky I am.' She took her son and began to feed him, and now the third day was over, she had more than enough milk to feed him naturally. 'Are you two going to the party tonight?'

'Who told you?' said Sally Ashford. 'Can't we keep any secrets in this place?' She laughed. 'It's really a royal command. They make it easy for us to be off but expect everyone to attend.'

'I know who you're going with, Nurse Ashford.'

'That's more than I know,' said Charlotte. 'Is Brian coming?' she asked, quickly.

'No, and I don't know what Mrs Taylor is talking about. I'm not going with anyone but the nurses.'

'That nice student who did the breech baby said he was taking you.'

'He did?' Sally frowned. 'I remember joking about it, but I can't remember saying I'd go with him.' She went back to the nursery with Charlotte. 'I suppose we can all go together. I don't want to go there with any particular man. You know what this place is like. Eyes everywhere and two and two making six.'

'Does it matter? I like to stir it up sometimes. Give them something to talk about . . . makes some people live a little through others.'

'I'll bring Brian up here and you can take him on the Heath,' laughed Sally. 'That should make the tongues wag. I've told my family that you will be coming down for a weekend soon.'

'I look forward to that,' said Charlotte, 'But why the sudden aversion to anything in trousers? You aren't still sore at Matthew Tregonna for getting you wet, are you?'

'No,' said Sally with truth. Not for getting me wet, she thought, not for being rude on the ward, but I can never forgive him for tearing my heart across and thinking that I am a loose woman. I can never forgive myself for trembling at his touch, dissolving under his kiss and wanting him so desperately that I nearly abandoned myself to his embrace. 'He is in London and doesn't come into the picture here. I've almost forgotten his existence,' she lied.

'I hope you're right,' said Charlotte. 'There have been times . . . oh, skip it.' She picked up another baby. 'Why do they go red and smelly as soon as I pick them up? I changed you, you little horror, just five minutes ago and now look at you!' Tenderly, she changed the infant and wrapped him in a clean blanket. 'Have you thought that Mr Dillinger likes to see all post ops after a few days, even if he doesn't do the job himself?'

'Yes, he's very particular about it. Sister said he was in yesterday to see some gynae cases.'

'And on his firm, he likes his S.R.O.s to do the same. Digest that thought for the day and tremble, my pet,' said Charlotte, sweeping out of the nursery with a baby on each arm.

Sally almost stuck the pin in the baby she was changing. Matthew Tregonna would come at least once more to check on his Caesar! Of course, he might come when she was off . . . she had the next night off after the party and with any luck—or lack of luck—she would miss him.

The feeding round took all her attention as several of the new mothers found it harder to manage their own babies than they'd thought possible, and needed tuition, but the room where the newly delivered women were nursed sounded bright with laughter and joy and it was impossible to have her own dark thoughts for long in such an atmosphere.

Michael found her in the clinical room. 'All right for tonight?'

'I'm sorry, Michael, I'd almost forgotten it. Shall we all meet at a certain time and go together?' His face lost its smile. 'We can all be together . . . more fun in a group, don't you think?' She smiled. 'But I shall expect a display of perfect disco dancing. I'm terrific, myself, or I like to think so.'

He brightened. 'For one awful moment, I thought you were giving me the brush.'

'What brush? We've never had anything going, Mike.'

'No, don't get me wrong. Not like that, but I told someone I was taking you and it seemed to impress him.'

'Who?' she said, with a dangerous glint in her eyes. 'Not spreading rumours are you, Mike? I've had enough of Redlake gossip.'

'One of the patients asked me, when Mr Dillinger was here, and he overheard.'

'Well, he wouldn't be impressed one way or the other.' Her relief made her smile.

'On the contrary. He asked if you were the nurse who had assisted with Mrs Taylor, the nurse with the marvellous colour hair was how he put it, although how he could know what colour hair you have when you were gowned up and he wasn't even there, beats me.'

'He's seen me at Beatties,' she said.

'Seemed to think I was lucky to be taking you and asked if I had known you for long.'

'Checking up on you and making sure you didn't waste your time in idle dalliance,' she said.

'No, checking up on you, I would have thought. Don't tell me the old man's cradle snatching?'

'If you as much as *hint* that, even in fun, I shall refuse to have anything to do with you tonight.'

'Only fun,' he said, plaintively.

'Well, watch it. And remember who it is that

helps you out of corners when you can't fix a nappy or bath a baby.'

'Mercy, and I swear I'll never tell your dark secret,' he said. He grinned. 'But the way you carry on makes me wonder just what is going on in that pretty head.' His glance swept over her slim body and lovely face. 'And it is a pretty head, and everything else is pretty too. Somewhere, someone is a very lucky man, or will be when you lose that very small chip you carry on your shoulder.'

It seemed as if the unit knew that the staff needed a break and for the rest of the night there were no admissions, no deliveries and no panics. At four, Michael insisted on making porridge, saying that it was the best thing for early morning inertia. He ladled huge spoonfuls out into bowls in the unit kitchen and poured syrup over it. 'Now I know why you volunteered to put on the breakfast porridge for the patients,' said Sally. 'It is good and I was getting a bit low on calories.' She giggled. 'My family would never believe this. A ward full of sleeping mothers, a peaceful nursery and an empty labour ward and me eating this stodge at four in the morning and enjoying it.'

It was good to feel that she could go through the day knowing that she had a night off and there was no need for too much sleep during the day. She saw a flurry of rain against the ward window and hoped that it would pass so that she could go for a walk, and when she went off duty, the sun shone on freshly washed leaves and the puddles were drying fast.

'Come and play tennis,' said Charlotte. 'I need exercise if I'm to fit into my one and only dress tonight.'

'That's a lie,' said Sally. 'You've more clothes than the rest of us put together. I wish I had some as nice as the one you wore to the last do at Beatties.'

'Rubbish,' said Charlotte with the confidence of one who knows her clothes are expensive and in good taste. 'What are you wearing?'

'I don't know. Just a shirt and summer skirt. It isn't very formal, is it?'

'Such abysmal lack of interest. I shall make sure you pretty up and enjoy yourself. Lately, I've noted a certain lack of *joie de vivre*.'

'I'm all right, Charlie. I just don't feel like cavorting about to convince Matron that I like it here, even though I am enjoying it more than I thought possible. The tales we heard about this place are true in part, but it's people, not buildings and equipment that make a hospital work well and happily. We've a good crowd at present and I shall miss them when we go back to Beatties for the rest of our time.'

'We still have a few cases to do before we go back. I shall keep my notes long after I need them for the record, to remind me if I ever get big-headed just what it was like being a pupil midwife.'

They walked on the Heath as far as the monument and looked down at the view of the neighbouring town that looked far away—a cosy mass of warm red bricks interspersed with trees and flowering shrubs. 'It's strange how little we use the town,' said Sally. 'We work hard and this walk seems to be more satisfying than taking a bus and looking at shops. It's a beautiful place.' They came to the second pond and sat for a while under the beech trees edging a tiny copse. 'This is better than tennis, today. I really haven't the energy if I'm to sparkle as everyone seems to want me to do this evening.'

The main road wound from the town through the Heath and beyond. A steady stream of traffic reminded them that there was a big flower show a few miles away and that some people were going on early holidays. Sally watched the cars as they walked back by the pub and wondered if the black limousine that purred along in the direction of the hospital was one belonging to a consultant. Her heart beat faster. No . . . there were hundreds of estate cars with a similar colour to the following car . . . a similar film of dust, and it was silly to imagine Matthew Tregonna behind the wheel, even though the back of the man's head glinted into gold as the sun found it through the glass. The estate car followed the black one.

Charlotte wanted to check the post in case she had a letter from her mother about her birthday. 'She insists on giving a dinner party every year, which is one way of making sure we all toe the line and pay homage.' She sighed. 'I shall have to go there and meet the whole boring set who make up my family's circle, but I have no intention of letting it interfere with my visit to you.' Sally tried to hang back. 'Come on, you might as well see if there's anything for you.'

They walked to the front of the nurses' home where the drive faced the car park and Sally averted her face as she passed, hoping that the car had gone and she had made a mistake, and yet longing to know that Matthew was in the building. The car was there, but there was no driver. She made no comment to her friend and collected her letters. If he was at Redlake, he might see his patient, perhaps stay for lunch with his opposite number and go back to London during the afternoon. She left Charlotte and went to her room to read her letters. 'Thank you for the harebells,' her mother wrote. 'They are perfect for one picture I am doing of all small flowers and grasses. If you could press some more and bring when you come home, it would be good. Alternatively, could you bury some in silica and I could use them in arrangements?'

Pressed flowers . . . flowers pressed between pieces of paper torn from a prescription pad. It was a joke, something to tease her with if he met her again. It was easy to take flowers from her as she slept, like candy from a baby or the virtue of a woman who didn't guard it well and wasn't able to protect herself from every good-looking man who came along—Dorian Warner, Brian . . . Matthew Tregonna. And if he heard the rumours, he would believe she was interested in Mike of all people . . . silly, dear old Mike who had about as much macho as a broad bean.

She slept lightly for four hours and showered, wishing that she could be more enthusiastic about the evening to come . . . and everything. Violet looked in when she came off duty and wanted her to look at a dress she had bought. Sally tried to be helpful and made a slight alteration for her to make it fit more snugly on her rounded hips.

'Thanks a lot. It makes all the difference. What are you wearing? I could press it for you when I press this seam.'

'I haven't thought, Vi. I'm too tired to go.'

'But you've just had a nice sleep. I looked in and you were far away. Come on, you can't let us all down like that.' The dark brown eyes looked anxious.

'All right, don't fuss, Vi. I'll come for a while and slip out if I'm too tired.' She went to her wardrobe. 'I didn't bring much with me.' She frowned as she pushed the clothes along the rail.

'What about that? I haven't seen that,' said Violet.

'Oh, I've never worn it. I bought it for a swish party in Bristol and then had the flu and couldn't go. It was a big mistake and I haven't put it on since.'

'It's beautiful,' said Violet. 'Just look at that colour.'

'I know . . . I was pushed into buying it by someone as bullying as you. I think it's too bright for me.'

'Bright? What's too bright?' said Charlotte.

'Oh, not you as well! Get lost, the pair of you, and I'll dress up in my good suit.'

'Oh, no you don't.' Charlotte took the dress from her. 'It needs pressing.'

'Give it to me,' said Violet, triumphantly. 'I've

got the iron on.' She hurried away with the slender slip of jade green silk and the floating scarf of matching chiffon.

'I shall look terrible,' said Sally.

'You *want* to look terrible, don't you? You don't want to enjoy yourself and you hate the thought of a party . . . you really need a good smack.'

'I'm sorry,' said Sally. 'I'll try and be good,' she said, meekly but with a slight return to good humour.

'That's better. Had your bath? That's good. You'll need different make-up to go with that colour and I'll give your hair a good brushing. It will buck you up more than anything.'

'I feel like Cinderella going to the ball,' said Sally, drowsily. 'What a waste. All this trouble for Matron and a few students and the spotty registrar.' But when she looked in the mirror, she saw that Charlotte had made her hair gleam with red lights and let it fall in thick richly coloured swathes. Tiny stars of silver were pinned cunningly as if they had fallen at random from a starlit sky and when Violet came back with the dress, she gasped.

'That really is something . . . you look like a film star, Sal.'

'Which one? Donald Duck?' said Sally, viewing her reflection with reluctant approval. She put on the filmy stole of kingfisher chiffon and noticed for the first time how the colour seemed to deepen and mingle with the jade silk as if their origin was from the same deep water or from the wing of the dragonfly. 'It's not bad,' she said. 'Thanks, you two, I don't know what I would do without you.'

Violet danced away to her own room to change, singing in a slightly off-key contralto. 'See you in ten minutes,' Charlotte said, as it was almost time to leave for the party. 'I think we shall be noticed if we arrive late. Why do I feel as if I am wearing my first party dress and want to rub the toes of my nice shiny shoes on the backs of my short white socks?'

'I know the feeling,' said Sally, but her heart was beating faster for other reasons. She ran down the stairs to the landing window that looked out on to the drive. Through the trees she could see the lights of the car park but knew that she hadn't a hope of making out the individual cars from that distance in the dusk. Perhaps he had gone back to Beatties. He was dedicated to his work and although he had such an irritatingly high opinion of himself, Sally had to admit that, as far as his work was concerned, he had every right to know his own worth. He wouldn't stay here for a party if he was needed on the wards in London, she thought. He had never been very happy about leaving Dorian in charge and a whole day away from Beatties was a long time in terms of obstetrics.

The night was clear and cool and the leaves on the tall poplars sighed languorously above the driveway and ripples of light showed through the top-most branches as the moon rose. 'It's almost too good to go into a hot, smoky room,' said Violet. 'A barbecue would have been better tonight.'

'The last barbecue I went to was washed out by a thunder storm,' said Charlotte. She glanced at

Sally, who seemed very quiet. 'You didn't have much luck with your picnic, did you?'

'It depends what you mean by luck,' said Sally. 'It served to cut down the time that Matthew Tregonna had to have me with him.'

'Oh, dear, I hope he isn't there tonight. Shall I call the fire brigade now to be in reserve in case you breathe fire all over the poor man?'

'Don't be silly, I shan't be difficult. I shall just keep away from him if he puts in an appearance. I know we don't get on well and he will have someone with him, in any case.'

'What makes you say that?'

Sally shrugged. 'It's common knowledge that he has no intention of setting tongues wagging about him. He's so sure that he doesn't want to be compromised that he takes a girl out once and drops her. I've had my turn . . . what about you, Charlie?'

The music was bright but contained and the group playing for the evening had strict instructions to keep down the decibels so that it would be possible to have conversation and not be deafened by the music. Looking round the room at the variety of age groups represented, it was fairly certain that they would have a wide range of tastes for which to cater. True to tradition, Matron was escorted by a surprisingly brisk chief surgical consultant who obviously loved dancing. They began the dancing and other couples drifted on to the floor to join them.

'Crikey . . . she'll have a slipped disc if he bends her backwards any more, but they seem to be hav-

ing fun,' said Charlotte, before being whisked away
by the house surgeon on geriatrics. 'I make him feel
at home,' she whispered as he came towards her.
'He feels safe with a poor old soul like me.'

Sally smiled. Charlotte looked very pretty and
was in the mood to enjoy herself. Michael claimed
Sally as his partner, apologising for not knowing the
steps to the ball-room type of dancing. The music
changed as Matron walked back to her seat, breath-
less. Disco dancing began with some hilarious
action by Mike, who hammed it up to make Sally
laugh. Her cheeks regained some of the colour they
had lost over the past few days and she managed to
smile as if she was enjoying herself. It's easy to be
like this, laughing on a superficial level, but from
time to time her eyes gave her away as she looked
towards the doorway.

'Looking for someone?' said Michael.

'No, just wondering who was coming. I didn't
know there were so many doctors here,' she said.

'Quite a good bunch and there's a few from London coming.'

'Who?' She dreaded the reply.

'Oh, I don't know. Some of Beatties were playing
rugger here this afternoon and what's left of them
are going to limp along later. I gather they drew . . .
bruises and all.'

'Oh, if it's a rugger crowd, they'll line the bar and
that's all we poor girls will see of them.' It was a
relief to know that the team was the only crowd
coming from London. She relaxed, determined to
dance until she was exhausted, without having to be

on her guard in case he came. The music changed again and the lights went soft. Matron was dancing a waltz with the chief psychiatrist and Mike groaned. 'You needn't do this, I'll let you off. Reserve your strength for the Reggae.' Sally turned to make a way between the couples and felt a light touch on her arm. Without looking round, she knew who was there and the thrill of awareness made her stumble.

'Careful . . . I know some people are all feet, but I'm sure you can do this with as much skill as you did the last curious dance.'

He held her slightly away from him as they danced, their steps fitting perfectly as if they danced in a film dream sequence. The chiffon stole swirled about them in a spiral of mist and the warmth of his hand through the thin silk at her waist drew her closer, into an embrace that was full of exquisite fear. She fluttered her eyelashes and saw his face, strong and expressionless above her. He saw the troubled look in her eyes. 'Why do you hate me, Sally?'

'I don't hate you . . . you showed me what you thought of me.'

'Every time we meet, you put up a barrier, except that one time by the river, and even then, after the storm, you showed me plainly that you wanted nothing more to do with me.'

'But I knew what you believed. You said as much.' He led her to the edge of the circle of light and out of the room. 'You saw me with Dorian and knew that Brian wanted to marry me. You probably even heard rumours that I was going out with Mike, the student I was dancing with just now, and you thought I was cheap enough to let you . . . that day by the canal you tried to . . .'

He was taking her away from the hospital under the dark velvet sky. She wasn't conscious of her feet touching the ground as, miraculously, she walked between the patches of bracken and heather. There was no way of knowing where he was taking her . . . no way of resisting his gentle progress, with his hand guiding her further from the lights and the music. 'Correction,' he said in a voice that held laughter as well as tenderness. 'Silly girl . . . frightened of shadows. Do you really believe that I intended any harm for you? Even if the thunder that broke up what was becoming a very satis-factory meeting had come much later, you would have suffered nothing at my hands, my darling.' He stood with her by the lake and the pale faces of the waterlilies glowed under the moon like the face of the girl who couldn't meet the gaze of the man who towered above her, one man who could sap her resolve, and yet she couldn't accept that he might want her as anything but a woman to be used and discarded.

'You know nothing about me except what you have seen on the wards and that one time in the car,' she said.

'And that was hardly a success, with both of us cross and wet through after what might have been a lovely day.'

She stood away from him, even though he had

made no attempt to kiss her. 'You haven't a very good opinion of me, have you? You know nothing about me as a private person.'

'I like your dog,' he said. 'That's a beginning. And he likes me, which might prove something. All right, I know, he can't tell the difference between friends and tramps.'

'I'm sorry if I was rude.'

'So you should be. I don't go round picking up young women and seducing them as a hobby. I don't go round picking up strange women . . . full stop!'

'I heard that you never took a girl out twice.'

'Quite true. I never need to double up.' He grinned. 'Always plenty of willing and eager girls waiting.' She heard the banter in his voice and couldn't see the amused sparkle in his eyes.

'There, you are so conceited, I was right to think you only looked on me as one of a sort of . . . pool of escorts for your passing pleasure.' She moved away, restlessly, her hands tightly clasped together.

'I'm beginning to think you have no sense of humour,' he said, 'And yet you seem to find other people amusing.' His eyes lost their softness and glittered coldly in the moonlight. 'You seem to be able to accept teasing from other men . . . and a lot of rather unladylike horseplay without getting annoyed, but if I say anything to tease you, it is different. I thought tonight that you were pleased to see me, after the first shock of finding that we could dance together had worn off, but now, I repeat the question I asked earlier. Why do you hate me, Sally?'

There was a rough edge to his voice and repressed emotion in his eyes. Against the moon, his hair was like a nimbus of gold . . . his face like that of an avenging angel. The moon shivered as a cloud passed over her face and the surface of the pool lay dull and devoid of life. Even the waterlilies seemed to lie deeper in the water with their waxen blooms half closed. Sally gave a sob and ran back in the direction of the lights. Her scarf flew behind her like the frightened wings of a dragonfly and the ends caught on a bramble, tearing the delicate fabric. She rushed on, dragging the scarf free and nearly falling. She put out a hand to save herself and touched cool grass, cool flowers. Her fingers closed over a tuft of something growing as she pressed on the ground to give herself the impetus to stand again. The scarf hung limply and ragged behind her and when she reached the bright lights, with the echo of a voice calling her to stop, she saw that she held three harebells, some torn grass and some earth.

CHAPTER ELEVEN

'I FEEL like a stranger,' said Nurse Sally Ashford. She looked round the immaculate ward and saw not a single face that she remembered. In terms of time, she had been away from the midwifery unit at Beatties for a short period, but in terms of patients being admitted, delivered and transferred to other convalescent places, it was at least two complete changes of bed patients.

'You've hardly been away. No time for anything of interest to have happened to you,' teased Nurse Cary, the staff midwife in charge in the absence of Sister Beringer.

'If only you knew,' said Sally, trying to smile, and Cary laughed. 'I did several of my deliveries and helped with a Caesar. We didn't learn as much theory as we do with Sister Beringer, but we liked it there better than we thought we might. In fact, the others were sorry to come back when we heard that the throat swabs were clear and the other three pupils could go back on duty.'

'And you? Were you sorry?' Sally shook her head. 'Well, it's good to know that some of you prefer us.' Cary gave her instructions about the nursery and brief notes on each of the patients. 'Remember Sandra? She took her baby to the annexe.'

'Yes, I saw her and asked her what she was going to do.'

'She came back here, full of plans. She is quite serious about keeping the baby and even considers getting married. The father came to see her, much to her surprise, and she gave him a good telling off.'

'Didn't that drive him away?'

'No. It was very funny. Sandra kept saying that she was going to bring the child up herself and he needn't think she would want anything from him! He got quite mad and began to say it was his baby and he'd be the one to decide that. Little madam, I think she planned it. She knew that if she pretended she wanted nothing more to do with him, he'd come running. I think we shall get a piece of wedding cake soon.'

'And they all lived happily ever after,' said Sally.

'Do I detect a note of bitterness?' Cary gave her the drug-cupboard keys. 'I'm off to lunch,' she said. 'Wait for me to come back and then take the other two. Sister is off all day and we are expecting two cases this evening. They have telephoned and are in early first stage—first baby for both of them. If they come in together, you can deliver one and Violet Bastable the other while I supervise.'

Sally walked round the well-remembered ward and into the corridor leading to the labour unit. It was good to be back. She looked at the shafts of light, cutting the white wall into silver and grey, and felt the peace of a well-ordered establishment. The corridor was silent, almost like a cloister. I suppose

I shall become like a nun, with important work to do, good work to fill my life, leaving no room for regrets or false hopes of love . . . romance. She walked back into the ward and talked to the patients. It was bad to be alone and to have time to think of the night of the party when she had to go back to the nurses' home to tidy herself and remove the scarf pinned to her silk dress, after she had torn it on a bush, fleeing from the man she loved and could not understand.

'Did I really act like that?' she murmured.

'What did you say, Nurse?'

'Oh, nothing . . . I was thinking.' She made an effort to talk and to show an interest in the women as individuals and not as bodies in beds, waiting for their babies or recovering from having them. It had been such a relief to be told the morning after the dance that she would be returning to Beatties in a day or so where she wouldn't have to face the curious glances of the staff at Redlake who had seen her return to the party, flushed and slightly rumpled, without the elegant chiffon that had been such a feature of her dress. It would have been better if I hadn't returned, she thought, and felt herself blushing at the memory of Matthew Tregonna sitting watching her, as one student after another danced with her. She knew that her cheeks were flaming with colour, her eyes over-bright and her laughter forced and possibly loud, but she couldn't turn to face him, go to him and say she had been a fool to run from him on the Heath. He sat without smiling, without seeming to see any of the dancers, and after a while she glanced fearfully in his direction. He had left as quietly as he had come when first he asked her to dance.

I shall never see him again, she thought. He went on leave and nobody seemed to have heard where he was going or for how long. The replies to her applications for second-part midwifery arrived and she and Violet were accepted by a good school. It seemed so long away . . . there was quite a while before they would finish part one and Beatties would hold sad memories as well as the good ones concerning her work. Where will he go after leave? He may not come back here at all. Mr Dillinger had told Sister that Mr Tregonna had been offered a senior registrar's post in the West Country, but Sister didn't know any details.

'Well, well, look who's here.' Dorian Warner grinned and followed her into the office. 'Thrown out of Redlake, were you?'

'No, we weren't. The others got better and we came back.'

'The others . . . has Charlie come back, too?'

'Yes, all three of our lot, but we all did some deliveries.'

'I'm leaving soon. This place isn't what I was used to down South. No scope for an up-and-coming genius in a place like this.'

'You mean that Mr Dillinger didn't take to your ideas, I suppose, and you feel . . . redundant?'

His face darkened. 'He doesn't know everything. He thinks he's God.' He wandered away to look for more willing ears for his grumblings, muttering that

Tregonna was no better and the sooner he left the better. Sally couldn't bring herself to ask him if he knew when Matthew Tregonna was leaving, but everything gradually pointed to the fact that he was going, if he hadn't indeed seen the last of Beatties already. One morning, Mr Dillinger brought a doctor to meet Sister Beringer, introducing him as the future registrar. It was all happening so quickly. It seemed impossible that the summer was not over and yet she had met Matthew Tregonna, fallen in love with him and driven him away before the first roses had dropped their petals.

'When do we go to Bristol?' said Charlotte.

'Are you off this weekend?' Charlie nodded. 'Good. We can go down on Friday night and if we have Monday morning off we can travel back by first coach. I'll ring my family and tell them,' said Sally. 'I could do with a break and we can spare this time from studying before we really get down to hard work.'

The rest of the day dragged until the two women were admitted, almost at the same time, and after that every member of staff seemed to be racing against time. The babies came long after Sally and Violet should have been off duty, but they stayed to complete their cases and went off duty, weary but happy, at twelve o'clock. If I could feel as happy as this through my work all the time, I could stand it, thought Sally. The sight of a young woman with her first baby in her arms was something almost holy, a private experience in the sharing of which Sally felt humbled and privileged. The hard work was forgotten and only the joy and fulfilment remained, to stay with her until she fell asleep, to face her ever-recurrent dream of a man with thick fair hair and smouldering blue eyes looking at her with a mixture of sadness and anger.

Nobody had heard of the holiday destination of the elusive doctor and Sally couldn't show too much interest in him after rumours had filtered back to Beatties of the night of Matron's party when Sally Ashford had come back from a walk on the Heath with Matthew Tregonna, flushed and upset, with her dress torn and rumpled. Even Charlotte couldn't find out just what had happened. 'This weekend is exactly what we both need,' she said. 'We worked hard at Redlake and haven't once had full off duty since coming back to London. The country with this lovely sunshine will be quite delicious.'

'I was caught in a thunder storm the last time I went there,' said Sally, 'But it will be fun to take you on the tourist trip round our ancient city.'

'What about asking for a lift?' said Charlotte.

'Never again,' said Sally, firmly.

'It wouldn't be Matthew . . . we could find out who was offering first.'

'I'd rather be under no obligation to any driver. The coaches are cheap and regular.'

'Suit yourself. I don't care if we have to hitch. I just want to walk in the woods and meet your family.' Charlotte had a gleam in her eyes that hinted of an unusual excitement. 'I want to look down into the Gorge and have a drink in the oldest inn in Bristol, and see the view from the bridge.'

'And meet Brian?' said Sally. 'Don't expect too much, Charlie. He's a pet, but I'm not in love with him and there's no reason why you two should even like each other.'

'I wasn't thinking about him,' said Charlotte, with an irritating smile.

'What gives? You look very mysterious.'

'Claud asked me to bring your mail along as we'll be leaving soon.' Sally took the letters and a small package from her, examining the tiny box-shaped parcel with curiosity.

'Looks like a sample of perfume or something similar. I'll open it later.' She tucked it into her handbag and gathered up her bundles and soft suitcase. 'We'd better be on our way,' she said. The taxi was waiting and as they paused at traffic lights or got caught up in traffic jams, they sighed for fresh air and the less busy streets of the country.

The motorway unfolded like a grey ribbon threaded through pale bridges, jewelled with amber lights as dusk fell and the passengers in the coach drowsed and dimly saw the flashing hedges. To be going home was good, but a cold corner of Sally's heart couldn't let her be free to look forward to it as much as usual. If he came back to the hospital while I was away . . . if he came just for a few hours and even mentioned me and I wasn't there . . . if he had one thought, one moment of anguish for me, I could live in hope that he might want me as much as I want him, and know that I love no man but him.

She remembered the box and opened it. Inside, on a bed of black velvet lay a tiny brooch of gold with leaves of green enamel and flowers of harebell blue. Two small flowers, faithfully modelled as if they had just been picked from the Heath at Red-lake. Charlotte saw the brooch. 'That's sweet,' she said. 'I knew you were hung up on harebells, but I didn't know you'd bought that.' She looked closer. 'It's really good . . . you are a very extravagant girl.' She laughed.

'I didn't buy it,' said Sally. 'I expect my mother sent it before she knew we'd be down today.' She smiled. 'She was so pleased with the pressed flowers I sent and the ones I preserved in silica arrived as good as new for her arrangement, she must have seen this in a shop window and bought it on impulse.' She was still smiling as the bus stopped and Brian waved to them. She introduced him to Charlotte and they packed into his car with all the strange-shaped bundles that seem so essential to any civilised weekend visit.

Charlotte rubber-necked as they drove past the Council House with the slender gilded unicorns on its roof, the tower of the university and the winding hill up to the Downs. The sun slid over the horizon as if it had waited just long enough to greet and welcome them and birds fluttered high in the chest-nut trees in the dense leaf covering. 'I love it,' said Charlotte.

'We'll show the rest tomorrow,' said Brian. Sally smiled as if she hugged a secret to her heart. 'You look happy,' he said, but his manner with her was forced, recalling his lie when he had not told her that Matthew Tregonna had telephoned, and still conscious that the other man had turned the situation to his own advantage by collecting Sally early on the morning of her return to London. To hide his embarrassment, he gave Charlotte his full attention until he realised that he was enjoying her company for her own sake.

Brian stayed to supper and left the girls with the promise to collect them at eleven, take them for a pub lunch and take it from there. Sally listened to the conversation around her and fell in with all the plans the others made, but her secret smile made her aloof from them, as if she was there only physically. Her mother glanced at her from time to time and smiled, as if she understood. She showed them all her delicate pressed-flower pictures, arranged with loving care and skill. She made no mention of the harebell brooch.

In the morning, Sally heard a light tap on her door. Her mother came in with tea and sat on the end of her bed. 'You're up early,' said Sally.

'I heard the post-man and there was a telephone call.' Sally raised her eyebrows. Her parents had a telephone by their bed and her mother never bothered with the post until she was dressed and downstairs. 'Rastus missed you when you went back last time,' said her mother. 'Can you find time to give him a good walk?' She looked at the clock. 'I know it's early, but if you went now, you could take him up by the observatory and back before the crowds get there. Have breakfast when you come

back, or miss it and take a couple of buttered rolls
with you.'

'Good idea.' Sally stretched. 'It's nice to have
Charlie here, but I do want some time on my own to
have a good think.' Her mother smiled, under-
standingly. 'I'll get up now,' said Sally and flung
back the bedclothes. Almost like a conspirator, she
took the large dog out to the car and started the
engine, not slamming the door until she was clear of
the house. She wore no makeup except for a sub-
dued lipstick and a touch of mascara, but her hair
gleamed clean and bright and the soft pale green
shirt, open at the neck and tied at the waist, had a
flattering line over her bosom. Jeans and training
shoes seemed ideal for the morning run and she felt
more carefree than she had done for weeks.

The river softly pushed the tide down to the sea
with silver hands, scooping the water from the mud-
flats at the sides of the gorge and sending it running
down under the screaming gulls that came to see
what the tide brought down as it reached Horse-
shoe bend. This was a good idea, she thought. How
had her mother known that she needed this? Rastus
seemed to laugh at her as if he knew a secret and
couldn't hold it in much longer. She let him run free
and he disappeared behind some bushes. He came
when she called and they walked by the cliff top,
gazing through the trees at the wooded slopes on
the other side of the steeply cut gorge. The bridge
lay ahead and Sally stopped at the observation
point from where hundreds of photographs were
taken every summer of Brunel's masterpiece, and

the wooden house in Leigh Woods.

She heard a whistle and turned. Rastus was a fool who thought that every whistle was to call him. She called, but he had gone. She sat on a seat by the tall tower of the observatory and took out the apples and rolls she had brought, expecting at any moment that the dog would come back. She tore one roll in half and took a bite.

'Are you always hungry . . . always ready for picnics?' Rastus panted beside the man who held him lightly by the collar.

'What are you doing here?' said Sally, choking over a crumb and hating herself for being less than self-possessed. A firm hand took the roll from her and gave it to Rastus. 'He isn't allowed titbits,' she gasped. Rastus accepted the morsel and sat firmly before them, with eyes lusting after the rest.

'If we give him the other one, do you think he'll go away?' said Matthew Tregonna.

'It's fatal to give him anything unless you have an unending supply,' she said, recovering. She thrust a hand through her thick, glowing hair and looked up at the man who sat so close to her on the seat.

'I'm flattered that you came so soon,' he said.

'But you didn't know I'd be here.'

'Didn't your mother tell you? I rang this morning. I made sure I spoke to her and didn't have my message intercepted as it was once before.'

'She said nothing . . . I couldn't make out why she wanted me to take Rastus for a walk.' She glowered at him. 'Have you been blackmailing my mother?'

He laughed, his face becoming full of life and humour. 'I called once or twice,' he said. 'I'm working at the General as from next month and I needed to be here for a while.'

'Why does nobody tell me anything?'

'Perhaps they thought you would take fright . . . as you seem to do every time you see me,' he said, gently, as if a raised voice might send her flying away again.

'I'm not afraid,' she said, in a shaking voice.

'I see that you are wearing it.' He touched the tiny brooch that glinted on the right breast of the shirt.

'I wondered who had sent it, and then I knew it must be my mother.' She looked puzzled, but there was an impish gleam in her eyes, implying a lie.

'You give me credit for nothing,' he said, but there was an answering sparkle in his eyes. 'I searched through London for that brooch and the girl says she thought her mother gave it to her!' He took out a pocket book and opened it. 'I was haunted by the sight of a beautiful girl fast asleep because she was exhausted, lying on the Heath with a bunch of harebells in her hand. If you don't want my gift, give it back to me and take these.' He put a flattened and withered spray on her open palm, the blue flowers still coloured and tied with thread.

She touched them gently and held them out to him. 'You took them from me when I was asleep,' she said, and blushed.

His arms were about her and she could hear his heart beating, a heart that would be beating stead-

astly for her—in city or on the Heath—at leisure or
t work. His kiss was everything she had wanted
ince the last time they met, and as her lips parted to
ive passion for passion, she didn't know or care if
his was for a moment or for all time. As he held her
way, the crushed dried flowers fell to the ground.
You knew that I kissed you as you slept, you smiled
nd stirred. Why will you never believe that I love
ou and want you . . .' his kisses were light and
unctuated each phrase. 'Love you . . . want you
. . need you for ever, my stormy little dragonfly.'
'he dog whined and Matthew reached for the rest
f Sally's breakfast. He threw it into the bushes and
Rastus raced after it.

'He'll get lost,' said Sally, weakly

'He'll be back, but first, we've a lot of catching up
o do.' His lips found the gentle curve of her cheeks,
he throbbing pulse in her throat and the deep cleft
f her bosom, and in her eyes he read the answer to
ll his yearning. She took his head in her hands and
s she caressed the thick curling hair as it rested on
er breast, tears of relief and joy fell like a summer
ew.

'You do know that they can see us from the
Camera Obscura in the tower,' she said.

'Who cares . . .' he said, and took her in his arms
gain.

<u>Two</u> more Doctor Nurse Romances to look out for this month

Mills & Boon Doctor Nurse Romances are proving very popular indeed. Stories range wide throughout the world of medicine – from high-technology modern hospitals to the lonely life of a nurse in a small rural community.
These are the other two titles for February.

STAFF NURSE AT ST HELEN'S
by Clare Lavenham

When Nurse Melanie Lister leaves home to share a flat she is disturbed to find that Andrew Forbes, a new house surgeon, is to be one of her flatmates. She is determined to dislike him, so why is she so concerned when he falls gravely ill?

APPLE ISLAND
by Gladys Fullbrook

Paula's success in her final nursing exam coincides with her fiancé abruptly breaking off their engagement. To recover from the blow, she joins the Tasmanian Tourist Nursing Service – and finds a new life, and a new love.

On sale where you buy Mills & Boon romances

The Mills & Boon rose is the rose of romance

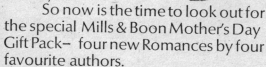

One of the best things in life is ... FREE

We're sure you have enjoyed this Mills & Boon romance. So we'd like you to know about the other titles we offer. A world of variety in romance. From the best authors in the world of romance.

The Mills & Boon Reader Service Catalogue lists all the romances that are currently in stock. So if there are any titles that you cannot obtain or have missed in the past, you can get the romances you want DELIVERED DIRECT to your home.

The Reader Service Catalogue is free. Simply send the coupon – or drop us a line asking for the catalogue.

Post to: Mills & Boon Reader Service, P.O. Box 236, Thornton Road, Croydon, Surrey CR9 3RU, England.
*Please note: READERS IN SOUTH AFRICA please write to: Mills & Boon Reader Service of Southern Africa, Private Bag X3010, Randburg 2125, S. Africa.

Mills & Boon
the rose of romance